The author

I0529743

Chris Page was born in Sweden in 1962, and brought up in Gloucestershire in the UK. After living in London and New York, he moved to Osaka in 1989, where he is based to this day with his family.

He is an editor, cartoonist, journalist, and copywriter, and supports all these occupations by working in education. Primarily, he writes fiction and dotes on his big, fat, black and white cat.

In July 2002 The London Magazine featured his short story, 'The Freebie'. That story is included alongside more of his short fiction in the collection *Un-Tall Tales*. Chris's novels are *King of the Undies World*, *The Underpants Tree*, *Sanctioned*, and *Another Perfect Day in Fucking Paradise*, all of which are published by Psipook Press and available from Amazon in paperback and Kindle.

Find out more at:

chris-page.com
psipook.com
or email psipook@psipook.com

Published by Psipook Press
Copyright©Chris Page
All rights reserved

Chris Page has asserted his right to be identified as the
author of this work

Second paperback edition, 2022 by Psipook Press

First published as ebook 2008 by Psipook Press
First paperback edition 2010 by Psipook Press

www.psipook.com
psipook@psipook.com

ISBN 978-0-9559588-4-7

The characters and events in this story are all fictitious.
Any resemblance to anyone or anything real is as
accidental as it is unlikely.

Cover and interior design by Chris Page

Weed

The novel.

Chris Page

Psipook Press

Now read on …

This is weird.

The telly seems to be getting closer. It is creeping across the room during lapses in Warren's concentration like an ingratiating dog or a stealthy predator. It also seems to be sprouting leaves.

Blaring primary tones, the tv is showing men stuffing wriggling, living sardines into their swimming trunks and chasing wailing bunny girl sirens around the studio while the audience howls, delighting in its own lobotomisation.

Outside the flat, in the sodium-stained night, the city pulses about as low as it ever gets: the police sirens are distant moor wraiths, and the screeches and growls of the elevated railway might be the distracted ruminations of Hell's teeth.

And the tv just shuffled a bit closer.

Warren — Warren Ladd, who incidentally adores from afar Sharon in Procurements — needs sleep. The week as usual has left him without rest, and this fast Sunday night is nearly done. Back to work in the morning. However, he is not going to sleep, he is not going to let the bastards take even more time from him. His employer, Daikon AirCon International, already has a great deal of Warren's time and has a contract to take much, much more in the future. It's not just Warren: they sap time from everyone they use; they are hungry for time — but then they are a growing concern and, time-wise, their nutritional needs are great.

They have now taken so much time from Warren they have left him like a rusted and seized old fob watch. So now Warren is stealing back time by petulantly refusing to go to bed at a proper hour and condemning himself to a miserable Monday dragging his hangover and exhaustion round the office. He's going to squeeze out the last of this weekend, he's going to wring it dry; he's going to leave the weekend like Daikon AirCon left his friend Bob Weed: all wrung out.

The monitor in the police Alpha Squad unit parked down the street is cruelly razored by a deluge of gamma emissions so that they have no idea what's going on. They have called for backup to get some triangulation going.

'Beats hell out of me,' confesses sergeant Testosteroni, fingers ineffectually skidding in the sweat-slick on his forehead as he tries to scratch himself. 'Either the whole damn city's sitting up and reading Grisham's latest or there's a hunk of plutonium nearing critical mass up there.'

Warren pops his thirteenth black bomber of the day, chases it with half a pint of vodka and hangs on for dear life, white knuckles on the chair's arms, bruising consciousness into his brain. Indistinct things scuttle the peripheries of his vision as if the room or his brain is infested with rats. The walls breathe laboriously and gush sweat.

'Wrrronnnggg!' booms Sam Smiles, the game show host, from his ivory lectern. *Bwaab bwaab bwaab* hoots the studio's sound system. The bunny girl has got it wrong. Her part in the quiz is to guess just how many sardines the guy has in his trunks. To be fair to the lass, it's a bit tricky, blindfolded and with your hand down the front of the contestant's shorts, telling what's what, with all that wriggling going on down there.

Warren wouldn't mind playing one kind of sardine game or another with the bunny girl. At a push he could even go for a game with just the sardines. Instead he snarls a big yellow-toothed snarl of derision at the tv and punches a finger through the tab of another beer.

Three floors above Warren the tv screams barely penetrate. On the bare wood floor is a fine detritus of tobacco and cigarette papers, flakes of ganja that missed. The occupant is relaxed, muscles uncoil from his bones and hang from his frame like untied ropes. Distinctions dissolve and he melts into the ether or the other of his self.

Back downstairs, Warren's television is definitely getting closer, but that's ok, just makes it easier to focus, and facilitates the omission of the world beyond the box. He is rocking violently in the armchair, bouncing the casters off the floor. There really does appear to be a whole bush bursting from the back of the machine. But that's ok. It doesn't seem to be after any of Warren's time or his vodka or his amphetamines.

The third Alpha Squad has arrived outside Warren's tower block and is reporting what the other two have already told Testosteroni, that the gamma emissions are overwhelming. However, together they have located the source in the Heavenly Estate, a brutal convolution of residential concrete blocks. Now they are hoping that the power of their combined suppressors will refine the signal enough to determine in which building and in which flat the interference is being generated. The Alpha Squads edge like wary cockroaches between the pillars of the estate. Headquarters is curious and has quietly positioned an Executive Action Group in the vicinity. Their dense, light-absorbing APC is like another shadow in the web-like fracture of streets around the Heavenly Estate. Inside sit the executives in stone silence — visored, cradling M16s between their knees; poised and priapic.

Three floors above Warren, our subject Robert D. Weed — Bob Weed; Weed; Bob — has finally keeled over under the enormous weight of his head. He is semi-foetal, half on, half off the thin mattress on the floor, his shoulders cloaked in the greasy grey-ochre huddle of his much unwashed quilt. His eyes are open but he does not see the living green patina on the damp plaster and the skirting board.

Weed has had a hell of a week too. While Warren is stealing time, Weed is simply all timed out: Daikon AirCon has taken so much time from him he has none left for himself. Being exhausted of his time potential, Daikon has thrown him away. Weed has nothing. Weed is nothing. He really is coming into his own.

Daikon has not only wrung out all the time in him, they have abused and humiliated him, mislaid his girlfriend, and stolen his home.

Weed has successfully remained stoned and immobile for the whole week. Stoned? He is out of his tree, out of the entire forest; he's on cloud 999. He is goo-goo and ga-ga, both. He is zonko doo-lally and flim-flam fnooberty boop, too. Never before has anyone been quite this stoned. Yes, indeed, Weed has scored some magic weed. Good job too, as there wasn't a lot of point in him hanging around on this planet to see the mess it was making of him.

The lad was expecting to be picked up by the Alpha Squads in the hour of his first smoke — the same Alpha Squads that cruise our cities for us, monitoring the alphas and gammas of our mind states, assessing our potential for riot, crime, our peace with our lot and everyone else's, our satisfaction with our jobs and our dinner, our contentment with the Alpha Squads themselves, and generally running to ground any unauthorised mental states that might suggest drug or literature abuse or just an exceptional sense of fun. However, the squads have so far overlooked Weed, and right now when he is traversing the starlit inner spaces of his mind and when his signature should show like a huge warm glow over the city on the police monitors, he is being shielded by Warren's frantic emissions.

In his present state Weed is primarily smile. He is good at smiling, he has been trained to smile properly, trained meticulously and thoroughly. He has been trained by his employer Daikon AirCon, who, in case you've never heard of them, make air conditioners. They are the guys who have the deal with the UN to end global warming by air conditioning the entire planet.

Weed was the lucky recipient of this invaluable training because he was an actual salesman. Well, perhaps the term 'actual salesman' is a slight overstatement. He was actually an actual trainee salesman, and not a very good one at that. For part of the week Weed worked on what the company liked to call the front line, on the floor of their big central showroom, the Daikon AirCon Human Communication Venture, but for most of his Daikon week he was required to work in the riskier, more challenging, and consequently more exciting spaces of No Man's Land — which meant selling door-to-door. In both these tasks, smiling was essential and the company had, in the interests of maximising the satisfaction of the sales experience for both their staff and their customers — about whom they cared deeply — altruistically incorporated smile lessons in the training schedule.

Recognising that the world contained an uncountable variety of cultures, races and individual types, Daikon's elite Human Communication Enabling Group had formulated four smiles which could be used safely and effectively in any nation on any continent — and were, daily and to great benefit for the coffers of Daikon AirCon. Behind this was the Otherness Overcoming Approaches Project who, after much painstaking research, identified four broad human types, each deserving its own special smile. The four groups were: people who clearly wanted an air conditioner, people who were unsure whether they wanted an air conditioner, people who were under the impression they did not want an air conditioner and people who thought they themselves did not want an air conditioner but who may know someone who did — into which category fell all children, hunter-gatherer tribes and domestic pets.

In each room of Daikon AirCon's huge, nebulous and space-age training complex deep in the countryside, overlooking an industrial estate and conveniently located to take full advantage of the copious rail and road links to the capital and other significant centres — Camp, it was called — were to be found four giant plastic smiles, each mounted on its own stick. Each smile was different from its three siblings; each set of four was identical to all the other sets. These were the models to which each of the student sales people, all the Joyful Encounters Division hopefuls, aspired — with varying degrees of success.

'Why are you snarling, Bob?'

'I —'

'Please, Bob,' complained Ms. Wap, his trainer. 'Smile, please! Take it from me, snarling does nothing for sales. It puts people off. And then they don't want to buy anything from you. I think you'll find that holds true of most products, Bob.'

'Yeah, I — '

'Do you have many friends, Bob?' asked Ms. Wap, full of concern.

'Well — '

'You'll find,' continued Ms. Wap, 'that people who smile a lot have lots of friends, Bob.'

A big blob of pink, gelatinous concern oozed over her collar and dribbled gloopily over the breast of her uniform. 'And when you have a lot of friends, Bob, the world seems a much brighter place and we find less and less cause to snarl which brings more friends and more happiness until we wonder why we ever bothered to snarl in the first place. And when we smile we make other people want to smile, and when they smile, still more people want to smile. Smiles are exponential, Bob. Do you know what exponential means? It means something gets bigger quicker than you would expect. And when eventually everybody in the world is smiling, Bob, there'll be no more wars. In this way Daikon AirCon is making a unique and meaningful contribution to world peace and harmony and understanding between races. Because we do business on all known continents.'

She cocked her small and perfectly oval head to one side and flashed a big number two smile, the one for people who were not sure whether they wanted an air conditioner. 'Ok, Bob?'

Concern in large pink jelly tears were evident on Ms. Wap's knees just below the hem of her skirt and were edging down her shins and calves.

And Ms. Wap really was concerned and not just pretending. Her whole life was her work. Her trainees were her reason for being, and as such, her concern was 24-7. Come the end of the working day, having seen her charges are — as close as she can manage without following each home — put to bed and tucked in and kissed on the forehead and well warmed on the inside with lots and lots of homework, she sets about her next selflessly efficient task of reviewing the relevant pages in her own trainer's training manual that will guide her through guiding the trainees through the next day's ream of their own training manual. Once finished with this she performs her next essential task, which is to minutely adjust all graphs and charts on their stands and realign all the big plastic smiles. This she appears to do according to some arcane protocol, according to some corporate-spiritual lay lines, inscrutable to all but the adept. In fact, this is nothing in the manual, yet before we accuse her of breaking the first rule of Daikon's employment code by acting on her own initiative, we must understand that the lay lines here derive from Wap's own cosmology and are in fact diversions or tangents that point away from the long dark night ahead; a night like all other nights packed solid with absence: the absence of trainees, the absence of people, of light, heat, love or life; a big ineffable nothing like the nothing before each of us were born, or the nothing before the big bang.

And now Ms. Wap has tweaked the last of the artificial smiles and ironed all the stacks of new documents — training report forms for her brood and lateness condemnation chits for her runt Weed — she has pruned and petted the plastic cheese plant and sung a little lullaby to it, and now there is no more to do but go.

She collects her pillbox hat and dachshund coat and clicks emptily through the Nuremberg foyer and through the big doors into the lack of day.

Ms. Wap lives in the Heavenly Estate, the same place Weed will end up, though you wouldn't have guessed it: she seems so other; too good for heaven; and she keeps the bite marks well hidden. Finally she arrives at her flat where the dark and the absence is packed even tighter than outside and makes the place seem bigger and less homely than the lobby of her office building. She eats a small but resolute meal, irons and fluffs tomorrow's clothes, does the housework, which involves fastidiously polishing every object in the flat although everything already gleams brightly with care.

Finally, in the smallest hours of the morning she showers, dresses, carefully puts on her makeup, gathers her files and briefcase and props herself against the front door, waiting for the day to come back, perchance to sleep, definitely not to dream.

'Ok,' said Weed, 'it's just — '

'Yes, Bob?'

'It's just that — '

'Why are you snarling again, Bob?'

'I'm not snarling, this is a number one,' the smile for people who were sure they wanted an air conditioner.

'It's not a number one, Bob, it's a big, ghastly, insane snarl. Trust me, Bob. I've been working at Daikon AirCon since I left school.'

Twenty-two, thought Weed, twenty-three? She had previously said she had been working at Daikon for six years. Did this mean she didn't actually go to college? Did she actually complete school? Anyway, he was getting her age pinned down. Not that much younger than himself.

'And all that time I've been working with smiles, Bob. Please trust me when I tell you that's a snarl, not a smile.

Learning the difference can be awfully useful,' she said, ever so reasonably.

Weed honestly did want to smile — if only so they could get this interminable training over with. However, whenever he tried, his face would contort into a foul rictus. It was just that these smiles did not seem to fit him; different smiles grew on Weed's face. And this he was going to explain to Ms. Wap.

'The thing is, Ms. Wap — '

'Oh, please call me Ms. Wap, Bob,' said Ms. Wap, 'there's no need to stand on formality here. Just Relax.'

'Why can't I just use my own smile?'

Ms. Wap looked at him with all the sympathy and compassion she might show a child dying of starvation. Specifically, she beamed at Bob all the compassion she would show a child that was dying in a country totally lacking modern infrastructure, which was ripped apart by internecine warfare, and whose population was almost entirely without air conditioners; a child that could have made the more sensible and considered choice of being born to different parents in a stable, wealthy country; a safe, middle-class country. It is all about choice: we are exactly what we choose to be and we should pity the poor souls who are unable to grasp this simple fact.

'Because I'm afraid your smile doesn't apply, Bob. I mean, it's a wonderful smile in its own way, but it isn't a three or a four and it most definitely isn't a one or a two. And it's just one smile, Bob.'

The luminous up-welling of concern evident at her collar and cuffs and hems had become a torrent, a slow-motion Niagara of pink blancmangey care.

'But mostly, Bob, our smiles have been developed in that most human of environments: the sales environment. Our smiles have been created and tested for your convenience, Bob. They're meant to help you. We just want you to be happy.'

'Yes, but — '

'You do want to be happy, don't you, Bob? You do want to work as a salesperson in the Joyful Encounters Division, don't you.'

No. Bob did not really want to be a salesman of any kind but right now the alternative was unemployment, being a non-person, and a slow death by starvation.

'You know, this is a most wonderful opportunity, Bob. There are literally millions of people around the world dying of rickets and scabies because they can't eat, who'd happily chew off they're own right arm to be able to be in your shoes now. You are select, Bob, you are chosen. Don't underestimate these smiles.'

She gestured at the big, shiny plastic models behind her on the presentation table. 'The Foreign Office and the Ministry of Defence — and others I'm not at liberty to mention even the existence of — are interested in our smile programme here. Anyone who can master these smiles will have the world at their feet. And it really isn't that difficult, Bob. Smiling is one of the most natural and simplest of human activities, which is why we've invested so much time and energy into our unique Daikon smiles.'

Ms. Wap went on but she genuinely could not understand that Weed was trying, that he knew what he should do but that he was simply incapable of smiling like he was supposed to.

The concern was dripping off her extremities and had escaped from her shoes to form a big sticky puddle on the floor. The other trainees would now be making mental notes not to step in this pink drool on the way out. They would be leaving translucent footprints all over the building and it would take ages to scrape off their shoes come the evening, catastrophically consuming homework time, and sleeping and eating time, and living and breathing time.

Yes, Weed wanted to be happy, he really wanted to be happy. He wanted to be so happy he could happy away all the wars in the world and then happy people into buying non-military and socially useful air conditioners, earning himself the while a big, robust commission which would make him happier still. But mainly he wanted Ms. Wap to be happy. He wanted to happy Ms. Wap. He wanted to happy her onto her presentation table and sweep away the big, red balloon smiles and the oral hygiene/sales fulfilment comparison graphs. He wanted to happy himself up her thighs and under her skirt, happy her out of her tight, corporately exciting uniform, happy all over her breasts, and happy inside her with all his new colleagues in serried ranks standing to attention, smiling happily on. That's how bored and fed up he was. He was so bored and fed up he wanted to get publicly intimate with a woman who had no apparent respect or affection for him, and with whom he had absolutely nothing in common. That's the kind of stuff that happens in a seriously bored male brain.

Weed became aware that, standing a pace forward out of ranks, he was standing to attention in more ways than one — and conspicuously so. Corporate trousers, without vents or pleats, and bottom-hugging tight, seemed to be designed to throw the smallest event inside your trousers into the sharpest relief. His face twisted in a big agonised smile — one that possibly deserved Ms. Wap's label of foul snarl — he wearily thought, nice one. Is this what Ms. Wap meant by exponential?

Weed thought that the main obstacle to his or Daikon's happiness as it touched Bob Weed was the company's own munificent concern for his happiness, and the planet's happiness, and its own happiness. Training had squashed and pulped every trace of enthusiasm he had for anything. In the pursuit of happiness nothing was left to chance by the company. The way you smiled, how you shined your shoes, what you said to the client and in what order and with what timbre of voice, was all bound by procedures and rules that were detailed in a seventeen-volume employee manual and were practised in training until they were second nature: or, more accurately, until they had entirely replaced the trainee's nature. The training programme was utterly comprehensive and attempted nothing short of a clean install of the individual's operating system. Weed felt he had rigor mortis while still alive: disillusion, frustration, and ennui had ossified his mind and every muscle fibre within him — Weed's happy johnny being the most blatantly ossified part at the moment.

'Do you?' repeated Ms. Wap, happily.

'Uh?' inquired Weed.

Wap had been talking to him through his reverie and he had lost his place in the conversation.

'Do you?'

'Of course I do, Ms. Wap,' he said sincerely and automatically.

For a moment, just the merest twinkle of a moment, the unfazable Ms. Wap seemed to fumble the strings of her smile but her recovery was immaculate.

'Well, I suggest you have a word with Mr. Stonewall in that case,' she said.

Weed wondered what he had admitted to doing as Ms. Wap announced an end to smiling for the day and suggested everyone stand at ease. The mannequins around him burst into a frenzy of massaging, trying to erase with their fingers and palms the imprint of winning smiles that Ms. Wap had neglected to cancel while lecturing Weed. Meanwhile, Ms. Wap made a note in the training log.

'Get it right will you, Weed,' hissed a voice in his ear. 'You're putting us all in the shit.'

'Right,' said Ms. Wap. 'Sluicing,' she announced.

Weed's interest perked up.

'First, underarm sluicing, then we'll move on to sluicing other hard-to-reach body regions.' Sluicing was almost as important as smiling and oral hygiene, and there were more graphs to prove it. Sadly, many people, however thorough about bathing, were unaware of the techniques of proper sluicing to the detriment of their careers and their standing in the community. The great thing about sluicing, Ms. Wap energetically informed them, is that all you need is a sponge, some soap, and lots of water. Weed's interest sank.

'I'm here,' said Sergeant Testosteroni's radio. The caller did not identify himself. He didn't need to. 'I'm going in.' Only one person announced himself in this fashion without interminable prefaces in police gobbledy-jargon.

'Understood. Will keep you informed. Out.'

It was Inspector Yard. Yard had arrived. Testosteroni was awed. Inspector Yard himself was in the manor. The inspector's catchphrase "C'mon, punk, make my tea" was so popular even Hollywood stars wanted to use it, but Yard refused to sell the rights, and Hollywood was forced to come up with its own inferior version.

'Shape up, you worthless scum buckets,' barked the sergeant to his crew. 'Man on the ground. Let's do it!'

In the boll of the night, by Shangri-la Heights, round Olympus Towers, past Avalon Hall and veering left before Elysium House, strolls a man: a round man, a big ball of a man with a football head, red cricket ball cheeks, a golf ball nose, and ping-pong ball eyes. He walks — or rolls — nonchalantly and slowly, going where the ramps and stairs and walkways and the rucked tarmac take him; trundling silently between upended supermarket trolleys; skirting charred and mouldering mattresses; avoiding the heaps of black bin bags; ignoring the novas of paint and the dead cat under his feet. His head is happily cradled by his ample, rugby ball shoulders, and a quiet smile is recumbent on his comfy face.

He is carefully ignored. A Community Cruiser — half bicycle cop, half main battle tank — ignores him, gliding away into the deep galaxy of Cuckooland Mall, with only the barest crunching of glass under its six wheels. Several of the smaller shadows ignore him, sidling without glances — suddenly empty hands thrust into deeply innocent pockets — into alleys and niches even the architects of the estate knew nothing of. Two dogs humping in the bones of a burned out Mini ignore him. The cateracted apartment windows overlook him.

On and around he aimlessly rolls on Dr. Bovver soles pounded by long use to the motherly consistency of old mattresses. He pauses to broaden his smile and to unwedge something from between his teeth with his right pinky. He looks up at the sour yellow sky while his big cheesy lips retain their moon. His brow divides and caterpillars over his eyes as if suddenly aware of something above or below or to one side of the usual range of human perception. In an instant he unslings an Uzi from beneath his left armpit and aims up at the still, blank facade of Nirvana Heights. There is a crash of breaking glass, normally as natural in this concrete massif as lark song in a forest, but this time too momentous to be a bottle or a car window. Some part of the estate's stressed structure has burst, and before the cascade of glass has splashed down, the round man has bounced out of its way. A siren bays, and the stroller, over the barrel of his gun, with his bright, swift eyes has picked out in the city's foul aura, high on the wall above him, something like drying laundry or a stray tree flapping in the hot wind.

Struggling vainly to get out of his seat, Warren swears horribly: his vodka is mysteriously out of reach. It is well beyond arm's length across the room. Or at least, so he thinks — it is getting difficult to see anything amid the thick animated shadows in here, and lying on his back, as he apparently is, he is suffering no little disorientation.

He pauses in his thrashing to get a handle on the situation and decides the main obstacle to getting up and out of the toppled chair is the tv, which is lying on top of him across his face and chest. Lying like this, he finds that he is cheek to cheek with a cow that is serving hamburgers in a burger joint. He is wondering whether he fancies the cow when he is invited to join a family who are wallowing in a bath of blancmange, and has to start wondering whether he fancies the mum and notices how the blancmange makes her look kinda multi-breasted like a dog or a pig. Something for the internet fetish pages, for sure. Next, he sees hairs tumbling from their follicles like Amazonian hardwoods and destroying the life of a perfectly respectable man as he is left bald. There was an advert for unemployment, a condition which could apparently be alleviated by having a job. Warren didn't fancy either condition very much. He did fancy Sharon in Procurements, who he adored from afar. However, if he was worried about his health he could take these complimentary pills that are as good for you as — and have been cleverly processed from — cabbages. One kind of pill will give you all the vitamins and minerals and the other will encourage regular and robust bowel movements. Saves you the bother of eating cabbages. If he needed some affection he could buy himself a baby. It comes in a miniature computer, and you can watch it thrive or starve on a tiny grey screen. It's as expensive and demanding as a real child, especially when it gets to school age and there are fees to pay and it wants its own pony and you have to buy extra software to stop it becoming delinquent but it doesn't look after you in your old age. The baby also comes in chicken shape or fish shape. There's a quick recruiting spot for astronauts. It seems people no longer want to go into space, and there's a computer-generated image of what space might look like if it didn't actually look completely different. Warren hasn't decided whether he fancies any of the heavenly bodies when along comes that cow again, now hanging out with the blancmange family, all basking in the breeze and a lot of sunshine generated by a funky little air conditioner on the living room wall. Makes flowers sprout on your carpet and fills the room with flappy little butterflies. He didn't fancy the cow or the bugs much, and especially not the flowers — not in his gaff anyway. His carpet already had enough problems with things growing on it. The daughter is way too young, but suddenly the cow looks pretty good. Uh-oh! In quick succession there are adverts for cheese, for plastic nose clips, for love, and for adverts. Better do something with the tv.

It turns out that this is no easy task because of the convolution of greenery that is filling the room and weighing on the box, but he finally succeeds in slipping out from beneath, only gashing his face on the stand a little and denting his head on a suddenly lurching corner. Once free, he burrows his way through the plate-sized leaves and thick stalks, gathering as he goes his cigarettes and stray beers, until he finally arrives at his bottle of vodka. He removes a limp and happy tendril of root from the neck of the bottle and wedges himself in a less cluttered niche where he possessively finishes what the plant has left him. Finally he lights a cigarette, thinks 'Weed' and abruptly succumbs to unconsciousness.

The round man handed the long thing back to the pyjama man with a big cheery chuckle.

'But what is it?' asked the small irritable man whose face was as grey as his flannels.

Vegetable, Inspector Yard had thought when the near hysterical fellow in the jimjams had given it to him. About a yard long, very hairy, pale and rooty in colour, one main trunk bearing several smaller offshoots and obscenely divided at the thin end. The thick end was roughly savaged with a sharp implement, a detail consistent with its finder's claim to have to have hacked it from a much larger growth with a kitchen knife.

'Know any wooden cats?' Yard asked.

'No ... '

'Well, it's not his tail then.'

'But what am I going to do?'

Yard had never seen such despair over a length of root before so he ceased chuckling a second and offered, 'Well don't try to pin it on the donkey 'cos I happen to know the donkey's got a cast iron alibi. You could take it over to the park and ask the trees there if they're missing any bits and pieces but they may send you to another branch.'

'Nah, come on ... '

'If you're going to beat the wife with it, remember to tie her up first,' chortled the big policeman. 'There're laws about that sort of thing.'

'But there's hundreds of them growing through my kitchen ceiling,' repeated Mr. Pyjamas. 'They're all in the cupboards and the fridge. They're all through the canned food and they've drunk the milk. Weren't there when I went to bed.' The man's lower lip was trembling. 'The wife's in a right tiz about it.'

'Better get it back to her then, eh?' Yard was about to turn away when he was overwhelmed by a sudden up welling of compassion. He put his big oven glove hand on the small man's shoulder and said in warm, supererogatory tones, 'Nothing to do with me, innit. Go see the estate manager in the morning.' He squeezed the man's shoulder and added, 'eh?' because it was friendly and he had forgotten to append it the first time through. Then he was off humming a little number about ratatouille and bubonic plague and rolling with his jovial gait into the black patches and tired lights of the tunnel under Nirvana Heights.

His breast crackled, 'Inspector Yard?' The big man hoicked the walky-talky from under his raincoat.

'What?'

'Alpha one, here. There's something you should know. Gamma's stopped. Back to normal. Just disappeared. No tail off — '

'Nah, the tail's off here,' tootled Yard, giving the grey flannelly man a conspiratorial wink.

'Erm ... ' continued Sergeant Testosteroni. 'Yeah, but now we've got something else: alpha. Abnormal alpha. Deep. So deep. So far off the screen we're having the same problem as before, only but the other way round.'

Yard re-pocketed the radio and treated himself to a full, derisory snort. He turned back to the small flat dweller, still uselessly dangling his yard of root at the tunnel's entrance. There was another sharp report from high up in the quadrangle outside, followed by the brittle glissando of glass. The worst occurred to Yard.

'You! Stay!' He shouted happily at the root man. 'And while you're waiting, don't hang yourself with that thing.' Then on the radio, 'Nirvana Heights underpass, west side, man with a yard of root. He's very unattached to it so be nice to the old git. Anyway, you might ought to want to have a word with him. No sirens. I'm going up.' And with a gleeful snigger, up he went.

Weed was in the office of Slater Stonewall HND, MF. The office was a transparent cubicle smack in the centre of a vast open-plan floor of clerks perched on high stools intent at computer terminals. So vast was this one floor, Weed could not see the far walls. Nor could he see the near walls. Every so often in the unendingness Weed could see other glass cubicles similar to Mr. Stonewall's or an occasional lift shaft or utility duct encased in perspex showing the pipes and cable mass that carried cool air, the data-blood of the company, power and sewage from one echelon of the organisation to another. There was a general hum of doing things, spiced with that ripping sound peculiar to office machinery. People conferred on telephones, sometimes apparently with their neighbours.

When he had arrived, Weed had found no sign of a door or a doorbell. He had knocked on the perspex wall.

'Always open,' was the reply. Mr. Stonewall was engrossed in a terminal display and was tapping keys on the keyboard without looking down. Weed could tap keys on the keyboard without looking down too, but never the right ones.

Uncertainly, Weed knocked again.

'Always open!' Then, by way of elaboration, 'the door!'

It seemed to Weed they were getting dangerously close to impasse when Stonewall finally looked up and smiled a number one at him. 'It's always open, my door. Come in, come in!' Weed went in.

'Robert Weed ,' he said, 'I —'

Mr. Stonewall leapt to his feet and sped round the desk with outstretched arms. 'Bob! Hi! So good of you to come!' He vigorously shook Weed's hand and slapped him about the shoulder a bit. 'Come in, come in! Sit down, have a seat! Take the weight off! No sense in senselessly wasting energy. We at Daikon AirCon are proud of our environmental sensitivity and commitment to sustainable development.' Weed stood while Mr. Stonewall shuffled chairs around, unclear which was intended for him. When one was finally prodded into his hamstrings he sat.

'Drink? Tea? Coffee?'

'I'm fi–'

'Gravity?'

'Oh, gravity please! Zero-G makes me throw.'

'Ah! A man who likes to keep his feet on the ground!' said Stonewall with delicious originality, and leaped energetically backwards into his own chair. 'I like that! You'll do well in business. And you *will* do well in business!'

Weed was not sure whether that was a prediction or a command.

'But,' exclaimed Mr. Stonewall earnestly, and earnestly flopping forward over his desk, 'all work and no play makes Jack a wee bit dull. You do play don't you, Bob?'

Weed wondered whether pocket billiards counted because that was the closest he had come to fun in the months he had been at Daikon AirCon. Fun just was not in it. The previous night was a frightening repeat of the many nights before it: he had arrived home late because Ms. Wap had graciously overrun a session on sitting appropriately when talking to clients. She felt that this was a crucially important skill and that the trainees would appreciate the extra practice. Huddled alone in her grey and empty little flat, the thought of all the selfless help she had bestowed on the peppy young trainees was the one little fire that warmed her spirit through the chill and solitary night until it was time to go to work again. Weed had gone straight home and arrived at eleven with a greasy fist of kebab to eat while he was doing his assignments. He found the meat was so hard and knobby he had to eat the kebab like a fly, first drooling over the thing to start a pre-digestion process, and then sucking vigorously on the tough knobs of meat and salad to haul the nutrients into his body through his own saliva. His assignment was to write an essay titled *Prolixity in interdepartmental, intra-discrete-functional-entity or colleague-targeted communicative expeditions; authorial consciousness of the same (a non effort -producing initiator is an unfocussed progenitor of corporate or personal initiatives); its concomitant circumcision; and the elimination of other imprecise things*, and it was due in the very next morning.

Weed passed out at two in the morning. He unpassed out at five still sitting at his living room/dining room/kitchen table with a charred cigarette butt under his tongue, covered in dismantled kebab, and clutching the sheets of his assignment, which he still needed to finish.

At seven, Weed lurched out of his chair, still wearing the same clothes and overcoat he had been wearing the previous night when he had come home, and barged out the door to get back to work.

The train was impossibly crowded and as the doors closed they sliced off any protruding bags, brollies, arms or legs, creating a clean, lean, no frills sausage of packed meat to deliver into town.

The crush inside the train lifted Weed's feet off the floor and as the train lurched on a bend his cheek made contact with that of a woman against whom he was crushed. Instantly, she screamed as if groped and turned an incandescent and very allergic red. It was then that Weed realised that he had failed to shave for the third morning in a row. Weed knew from Ms. Wap that not shaving was as conducive to a fulfilling and satisfying sales experience as having a poo down the client's windpipe. He had meant to shave; he really did not like not shaving and he wished not to antagonise Ms. Wap any further, but there it was: black, spinily loony evidence of his contempt for Daikon AirCon, or, in the better scenario, evidence of his pathetic incontinence.

And then there were his bowels. If Weed's relationship with Daikon AirCon was strained, then his bowels were at war with the company, and Weed was being shredded in the crossfire. In this routine of hurtling from one thing to another, his tubes just didn't have a moment to themselves. With horrific reliability they needed to do their thing five minutes after he left the house. He travelled to work with an industrial hydraulic pump installed in his person, which would leak on the train, seep in meetings, and become effusive in the face of clients. It seemed to Weed that even his biology was incompatible with Daikon AirCon.

'Because a sense of fun is crucial to the career of a successful salesmanperson, Bob. Crucial! Unadulterated seriousness dilutes the spirit and the customer thinks "what kind of colourless fellow do we have here?" They can sense it, it's almost tangible ... '

Mr. Stonewall had screwed up his face and was making clenching gestures in the air to demonstrate tangible but was better demonstrating unspeakable acts performed on an invisible little boy.

'Graphs show a clear correlation between spirit and sales fulfilment, Bob,'

Now Mr. Stonewall was tapping keys again with his eye on Weed who once again found himself impressed.

Not only could Mr. Stonewall operate a keyboard without looking but he could also read a display without looking.

'You do want fulfilment, don't you, Bob?'

'Oh, abso — '

'You do want a satisfying and productive life? You do want to be able to sit back in the twilight years and say I did the best that I could and that I wouldn't have done anything different, that I — I mean you — made the best of the one big, huge, unique opportunity that came your way: life; Daikon AirCon. No regrets, no failed adventures, an index-linked pension, which represents thirty-three point three percent of your finishing salary here at Daikon AirCon. Don't you.' This was presented to Weed in the commonsensical way that one might suggest a band-aid to a man who has just cut his head off shaving.

Fulfilment, oh you flighty, fickle thing, come show yourself! Here's Slater Stonewall's fulfilment; here's Slater Stonewall having a life. For the last fifteen years and the next twenty-five, here's how it goes.

At the close of the business day Stonewall will slip his laptop into its slim attaché-type case and on the way out will bump into a gang of similarly middle managers and will be enticed down the pub for just a quick one as he always is.

In the pub he and his chums will swap jokes about colleagues and juniors and genitals and tell earnest and amusing anecdotes that incidentally illustrate their superior competence, and they will eat sausage and chips before heading home.

Slater Stonewall lives nowhere near his place of work and certainly nowhere near the Heavenly Estate and it always takes him a long time to get home. The travel is ok because it gives him ample time to fiddle importantly with his mobile phone and his laptop and grab furtive looks at the cleavage and legs of the girls on the train.

His wife meets him at the front door as she always does and takes his brolly and attaché and puts them in the closet thing by the door. She gives him a very domestic peck on the cheek and bids him a prompt goodnight because it is late. She puts her husband in the closet thing by the front door with his brolly and attachée and goes up to bed. She will get him out of the closet in the morning and push him gently out the door and back to work.

'Well, I — '

'Because a human being is a special and unique thing, Bob. Have you ever thought about that?'

'As a matter — ' Weed had a lot of thoughts on the subject.

'Have you thought about the thousands, the millions of years of evolution — ever since the Big Bang in 1987, and even before that: physical, spiritual and intellectual evolution — that have gone into each member of the human race? Or should I say huperson race? Have you thought about the sheer, dumb unlikelihood of life at all, let alone intelligent, sophisticated life such as hupersonity, a species that can build bridges and tall buildings, fly to the moon, make computers and free market economies? I mean we have even harnessed the power of creation itself, the power of the atom! I mean, atoms, Bob! Things so darned small — ' he illustrated how small with his fingers and a crunched-up eye, 'things so darned small you need a scientist to see one.

'And right now, each and every one of us is the sum total of all that's gone before. We are born and we live with the advantage of this incredible wealth of natural history, because that's what we see here, Bob, the distilled pinnacle of nature; life and geology's competition of strength — cooperative conflict you would probably say — all this groundwork which has been done for us. And that gives us our own wealth of possibilities. We are each choc-a-block with talent and privilege because one of the most valuable of huperson achievements is the ability to pull ourselves up by the bootstraps. Somewhere after the primordial ooze, somewhere after the invention of fire and the wheel' — unspeakable acts on little girls — 'and probably about the time we understood what it meant that

Christ had died for our sins, we learned what it was to bend down take a firm hold of our bootstraps and give them a really good yank!'

'A what?'

'Yank, Bob, a really good yank!'

'Oh, I —'

'When you think about this, Bob, you see we were born to achieve. Don't you see that? We have so much possibility, so much ability: oodles and oodles of talent. We really are quite privileged. And we are each of us a nascent business empire with long, empty, yawning warehouses just waiting to be stocked with success and achievement — crammed to the high rafters with boxes and crates of the stuff because that's how we become fulfilled, that's what living life to the ceiling — I mean the full — is. That's where the word fulfilment comes from. It means being filled up.'

Weed thought of Doughnutland where he would take lunch.

'And isn't it a crime, Bob, when people let all that wonderful talent, that ineffable opportunity go to waste? Some people just can't see it. They don't get it. They laze away their lives in dreadful poverty and never do anything to better themselves. There are laws against it, Bob, natural laws: the laws of natural selection for a start. For example, the law that says that if you don't try, you betray hupersonity, give the finger to all the people in history who did try and who succeeded, who laboured and sweated so we could have Daikon AirCon. And another law says quite simply, if you don't try, you don't succeed. Are you aware of these laws, Bob?'

'I sup — '

'I can see you're a trier, Bob. A born trier and you'll go far. I know these things about people. It's a gift. Some people are born with these abilities. Some people aren't. Quite uncanny really. Sometimes I frighten myself. But for goodness sake, Bob — may I speak frankly?'

'Y —'

'Cultivate yourself as a well-rounded person, Bob. Of course work is important — the most important thing in your life. But don't forget there are many aspects to spirit — soul, that indefinable core of hupersonity; that which makes you you and not another person, that which makes you you and not a field mouse or a bat or an umbrella; that which makes you a salesmanperson — a darned good salesmanperson — rather than a workhouse flop.'

The description of Weed as a darn good salesmanperson inspired the following memory. It was Weed's first day in the field, in No-Man's Land. That morning he had been tested to see whether he had memorized his pitches and had stunned himself by passing. A Daikon AirCon van took them out to the Heavenly Estate — or as near as the driver would dare go. Weed hadn't yet moved there, he still had that to look forward to. It was a cold day, a very cold day. Weed was shivering inside his light summer jacket. It was June. Sales operatives in No-Man's Land were not allowed to wear warm clothes until September the fifteenth. People rolled around lagged six inches deep in duck down and polystyrene while Weed shivered and scuttled across Satori Plaza through the broken glass and dog poo, hugging files and catalogues, looking and feeling like a missionary among cannibals.

His beat for the day was Nirvana Heights and Transubstantiation Tower at opposite ends of the estate — four thousand and sixty five flats in total. Weed politely wondered of Mr. Scourge the field supervisor whether it was possible to get through four thousand and sixty-five flats in a six-hour working shift. He was told that six hours gave him five seconds per flat, an allotment that would increase because some people would be out. Weed was just about to be impressed by their mathematics when he realised that the time it would take to walk the kilometre to the first block had not been factored in. Nor the time it would take to walk up twenty-seven floors of stairs when the lifts were found to be not working.

Weed then figured that the time it would take to get from the first block to the second and climb the stairs to be in the right place for the second part of the shift reduced his lunch break to about ten minutes, and we were here ignoring the inevitable overrun on the first block. Then the supervisor took him aside and gave him a five-minute lecture (sixty flats) on dedication and flexibility in endorsing targets, which Weed took to mean he would stay here until the job was done even if it took all night. In fact, Weed estimated it would take thirty-three point nine hours to finish the assignment. His colleagues were either less mathematically alert or entirely unbothered. Weed expressed none of these computations aloud but his supervisor put an attitude hazard symbol next to his name in the roll book then cheerfully reminded the group that since this was their first time out and since this was demographically very much an F region, a more than fifty percent success rate was not mandatory but twenty percent was expected. On minimum wage fixed at six hours or twenty percent of total sales, whichever was lower, Weed was looking forward to the day no end.

On the exposed walkway at the summit of Nirvana Heights, puffed and with the climb-induced sweat freezing on his body, Weed had his first lucky break. Seven hundred and eighty-five flats behind schedule, the very first one on his list was a burned-out shell. Five seconds saved.

He leapt the few steps to the next and hit the doorbell. He looked at his watch counting off seconds. He rang again. There was stuff in the manual about ringing again.

'There's nobody here!'

Initial resistance: do not be deterred. There was lots of stuff in the manual about that too. Initial resistors always look difficult but they can be among the most grateful of customers. Go straight into the pitch.

'Hello. My name's Robert Weed and I wish to speak to you on a matter of some impotence. Importance.'

'You're another fucking air conditioner salesman, aren't you!'

'No — yes — I ...'

'Piss off, I don't want one. I've got no money.'

Is that a number three or a number four smile in this situation, Weed wondered, and trying to see through the peephole in the door.

'In these days of uncertain climatic conditions and less than pristine air, is it not worthwhile investing in a little security and reassurance? We at —'

'Look, I told you! I've got a gun here and I'm not afraid I know how to use it! Do you know how many air conditioner salesmen I've had round here this week? Why can't you bastards just take no for an answer? It's not as if we live in a hot country either. It's minus fucking twenty degrees out there and you're queuing up at my door morning, noon and night. Well, I'm not taking it any more, do you hear me, I'm not taking any more.'

'In the stifling dog days of summer when your natural biorhythms are disturbed and your appetite is impaired, and all your hard-earned income —'

The surface of the door erupted but centimetres from the end of Weed's nose. Reflexively, he toppled over backward in a dead faint as the occupant of the house put several more bullets through the door in a professional bracket pattern that would surely have caught Weed had he taken standard special forces avoiding action instead of his farsighted lapse into unconsciousness.

Weed was lucky. He suffered only minor shrapnel scratches on the face. The sole was entirely torn off his right shoe.

When he finally crawled out of Nirvana Heights on all fours covered in blood and crying, his supervisor put another attitude hazard symbol next to his name and an actual black mark just to be sure. The supervisor then leapt up the stairs three at a time, sold the gunman an A-100 SoopaKoola air conditioner, powerful enough to refrigerate an entire beef mountain and left him in tears.

'Take time off occasionally, Bob. Let your hair down. Sit down and watch a bit of tv from time to time for goodness' sake! Are you with me Bob?'

'One hund —'

'Good man. Now —' Stonewall was not only operating the keyboard and reading the display without looking, he was also apparently absorbing a weighty report lying the desk in glances between sentences. Weed was more impressed than he would consider decent to admit.

'Ms. Wap informs me that your performance in both training and sales is wholly inadequate. Shape up Bob or you're out of a job. You can go now. And once again thank you very, very much for coming to see me, because here in Daikon AirCon Human Resources and all over Daikon AirCon we care very much for you personally, Bob, and appreciate the tremendous work you are all doing in helping to shape the future as Daikon AirCon sees it.'

He was flashed a number one, his hand was shaken and was suddenly out of the cube and into the general office where he decided he really needed to use the toilet.

In the lobby of the tower block Yard was briefly stalled by four non-functioning lifts. Cheerfully he took to the outside stairs — they would anyway afford a better view of the estate and its plumbing of wells and catwalks.

Almost immediately he met people coming down, people mainly in their nightclothes or with nightclothes blossoming from the cuffs and unbuttoned fronts of day clothes. Many were carrying ornamental clocks, tvs, pets, children and other valued possessions. At the sight of Yard they halted their flight to be deferential a minute.

'Thank God you're here, Inspector Yard, sir,' they said. 'It's awful up there.'

And, 'Take care of yourself, sir. No telling what's going on.'

And, 'Good luck, Inspector, it's already had the Perkins at number 1,249.'

Yard waved in universal response and bounced up against the thickening trickle of refugees. At the fifth floor he paused. Where a down-pipe opened over a grate, a hairy member emerged and, twisting a little, disappeared under the railings and out into space as if the night were better soil. This hirsute embodiment of yuck was undoubtedly a sibling to the yard of root the grey pyjama man had been dangling outside a little earlier.

Yard unslung a large blade from a secret recess in his sleeve and swiftly lopped the root from the base of the pipe and went on up. Two floors further on he found the outside of the open, skeletal stairway curtained by dangling ganglia which he unhung with a long satisfying burst from his Uzi. Reloading, he bounded on. Next floor there was more, which he dropped without breaking his stride.

The sound of gunfire duplicated itself dozen-fold on the walls of the hemming towers until it reached Testoteroni's ears a full-bodied fire fight.

He had another unsuccessful go at scratching his greasy head.

'Yard,' he whispered in inert awe.

There was no sign of a toilet anywhere. Weed wanted to ask directions but everyone seemed so busy he did not want to disturb them. Hassled clerks pushed by with wheelbarrows full of computer printout, which they dumped into big wire bins placed at the end of each nest of work stations, from where sweating folk in cheap suits used pitchforks to toss it onto the desks of data input clerks — haggard looking men and women perched on high stools whose fingers worked at the keyboard like flocks of starved geese. The reams of paper data were allowed to spill into yet more wire baskets from where yet more young workers with pitchforks and shovels would load it into wheelbarrows again before transporting it to other wire bins. Printers screamed and gnashed their cogs, kettles spewed steam, young graduates with scrubbed lobster skin gushed coffee-tainted sweat.

Trying to pick out a person to ask, Weed settled on a composed looking individual with a balding head and glasses who was writing slowly and carefully on a quaintly old-fashioned tablet of foolscap with a beautiful and classically knobby fountain pen. As Weed approached, the balding man was set upon by a horde of brown-overalled operatives who came out of nowhere. They dismantled the computer he was not using and made off with the telephone. They lifted up and carried away his desk to the east and lifted his chair with him and his fountain pen still aboard and carried it west. More of their band swiftly arranged the surrounding workstations and clerks so that no obvious space was left.

'Downsized, innit.' It was Warren, who had suddenly appeared at Weed's side and who was muttering conspiratorially in Weed's ear. 'Outsourced, rationalised, streamlined. Efficiency boosted. That was Mr. Rogers. Mr. Rogered, he is now.'

Weed and Warren were friends. Weed was into astronomy, quantum physics, chaos theory, geology, wildlife, Marquez and Bach. Warren was into football, booze, girls, stereos, psychotropics and flash motors — and, especially, girl pop groups who had themselves photographed wearing flimsy football kit, waving champagne bottles and buckets of pills from flash cars. He had a recurrent fantasy about Sharon from Procurements, who he adored from afar, in the back of a sports car, wearing a football shirt and drinking champagne. Weed and Warren were the best of friends. Perhaps they were the best of friends only because they lived in the same building within three floors of each other and worked for the same company. Perhaps this was reason enough to be soul-buddies in the vast, dizzying universe of Daikon

AirCon. This was quite possibly reason enough to be soul buddies in this vast, dizzying universe.

'Happening to us all.'

'You got canned?' asked Weed with incredulity.

'Nah! I got a new job. Got someone else's job. On top of my own job. It was someone else got canned. Thirty-six someone else's. MDMA/E was the group that got it. Now we got it too, like; mental it is at work. Snowed under; up to here in it, innit. Started at eight yesterday morning. Knocked off at eleven last night and that was only after pleading period pains or whatever. Same again tonight, you watch. I got a few nights of the rag and then I'm going to have to think of another excuse.'

'Try telling them you have peristalsis in your intestines. That always works for me. They say "poor dear," tell you to wrap up warmly and send you home. Or say you have a rod in your eye. That's another good one.

'By the way, Warren, it's nice to see you but where's the bog? I'm going to rupture.'

'Just down here on an errand. Get a chance to get out, you go for it, know what I mean. Suck you dry, they will. Take your time about it, have a smoke, a coffee at that spot on the corner if you're quick. Drop in for an ogle at Sharon in Procurements. That Stonewall, know why he has no door on his office? Open door policy, bollocks. He just wants to earwig, know what I mean? Anyway, they won't let him have one. No budget for it. Just over there, mate. Where you see that yellow and black doobry going down like out of that film Alien? Just behind there. But watch it, it's where the pricks hang out. Have one for me. More than three shakes is a wank. See ya.'

Like an indifferent explorer in a bleached jungle, Warren set off to finish his errand. Weed set off on his own. Dismayed at his interview with Stonewall and fantasising about waking the next morning to find that he had metamorphosed overnight into a competent worker and red-hot salesperson, he failed to keep in sight the black and yellow doobry that marked his pit stop.

Confronted with a monolithic metal case he simply changed tack. Up against another he changed direction again. This happened a few times before his nagging bladder persuaded him to take a bearing.

He realised he had wandered into a broad, empty boulevard lined with the huge filing cabinets. Backtracking, he learned that there were dozens of alleys leading off left and right, all apparently identical and offering no clue to the route he took here. He had no sense of in which direction to find the office, nor could he even hear it. The cabinets were about four meters tall and were proving to be excellent soundproofing — if you happen live next to a motorway or an airport or a war zone or an ice cream van and happen to be thinking of insulating your home against noise, you might be able to pick some up cheap from Daikon AirCon because they've got lots.

After experimenting inconclusively with a few of the side streets he decided he was in an unusual predicament. He was hopelessly lost in a maze of monstrously large filing cabinets.

Well, he thought, a filing system must have a beginning and an end, and began reading the labels on the drawers intending to navigate out by following the numbers to the end of their sequence. Starting at 509600 - 936999 he worked back toward 000001 until the labels discontinued at 247000. They reassuringly resumed at A. Just six paces later with no toilet or office in sight they terminated at Z but restarted at a. After d, that series went abruptly to aa, got tired at ll, and set off again at a disconcertingly imaginative 4LOC-TUG 633 0000 43-D, passed quickly through COW/2 - D/CUP, and when it got to INXPLCBL/ HO HO HO Weed gave up.

In a further outburst of initiative that would have had Ms. Wap rifling through her training manual, he resolved to partially open alternate drawers on two columns of cabinets to improvise a sort of ladder by which he would climb to the top of the cabinet wall, get his bearings and navigate safely to the lav.

When he opened the first drawer he found it empty of the expected files. Instead he found a small plastic foetus swaddled in a sheaf of burger wrappers and laid on a bed of shredded tv pages. The foetus had for a headboard or gravestone a calculator, one of those desktop-sized ones. All the buttons had been prized off the calculator and lay around like broken teeth.

Weed was intrigued. This was something he could relate to. In his summer jobs as a university student he had worked as a filing clerk and had hated it. His days were occupied by arranging bits of paper in alphanumeric order and stuffing them into cabinets that were already overfilled by tatty, mop-eared crumples of paper. Everyday something would crop up that defied the system; something that just wasn't A or N or Z, that wasn't 1 or 500,000 or 545-486-424/B, something that wasn't a letter of credit or a letter of query or a letter of complaint, something which was specifically a document of conundrum, a memo of mystery, an epigram of enigma. Lumbered with one of these orphans, one of these abandonees — these children of Fagin, these cuckoo chicks, these *weeds* — Weed was forced to discover which was more hateful, the mindless, soul-sapping filing of regulation scraps, or the futile, soul-sapping search for a non existent location for the bits that were too obtuse or too unlucky to follow regulations.

It was in this job that Weed first learned that while surviving a mindless job is painful, surviving a mindless job that you actually have to think about is a medieval torture. He used to fantasise about filing odd things. He once broke a tooth and spent much happy time wondering whether to file it under t for tooth, f for fragment or o for ouch. Should belly button lint go under l or f for fluff or h for 'ha ha ha'?

Whoever was responsible for this bit of creative filing had gone several better and had let their imagination out to play way past bedtime.

He wondered who was that clever to have found the right place for them; who was smart enough, who was perceptive enough to have realised that just these things should be billeted here in this drawer together, that these bits should be together in this drawer and not in those drawers over there, nor in some drawers in Poltoratsk; indeed who was bright enough to have divined that they should all have been in a drawer at all? He thought he might want to meet this genius

Speculatively, Weed opened an adjacent drawer. In it he found hamburger buns with star maps carefully etched on their dry domes. The maps were apparently accurate, and had been carefully reproduced using a scratchy old fountain pen. The buns were laid out in the bottom of the drawer as if they were themselves planets in a star system, and at the centre of the system there was a larger pile of buns: the sun; the locus. The sun was wearing a pair of glasses from which insane eyes dangled on springs and inserted in the bread between the eyeballs was a pair of clockwork false teeth.

The meat from the hamburgers was in the next drawer. Like the bread, it was thoroughly desiccated and had the consistency of veteran drink coasters. A dried worm had been pinned to each patty where it curled like a spinal column or kundalini to the beef's brain. The meat was arranged on a large map of the chakras and was kept company by a small plastic superhero and a box of spent matches.

Another drawer contained the lettuce, tomatoes, pickles and french fries, all very nicely mulched with pencil shavings on which was growing a forest of fungi that was anaemic to the point of perfect whiteness, and which seemed to physically cringe with the sudden light. With their little bulbous heads on skinny stalks and unstraight attitudes, the mushrooms reminded Weed of a big crowd of people in the underground or in a department store.

Forgetting about both his ladder project and his bladder project, Weed began to explore the filing cabinets. He found fragments of religious tracts representing most of the world's great beliefs in their native scripts — Japanese, Chinese, Sanskrit — finger-daubed in ink on the inside of a drawer that also contained a power ball.

In other places he found: a small green triangle inscribed inside a lopsided circle on the front of a bus ticket; a crucifix painstakingly assembled from old cutlery, kitchen tools and sellotape; an illustration from the back of a cereal pack of a clinically happy family enjoying the barbecue set and camping gear they won just for eating breakfast, whose faces had been removed with a semi-sharp instrument; a stringless ukulele; a trilobite; a plastic banana; garishly painted women's office shoes; a novel from which all the words including the title had been meticulously removed with a razor; photos of kids playing happily and an ad for breaded turkey patties shaped like Disney Characters taped into the gates of Auschwitz — those gates which still bear the legend Arbeit Macht Frei; an empty pint glass, still smelling of beer and now containing a single dead flower head, a Hubble picture of two galaxies colliding and a picture of the sun with "C'mon punk, make my day," scrawled on it; a shopping catalogue whose cover of a genetically perfect pair of models walking hand in hand had been amended with a homemade speech bubble in which the woman said "If you buy this dress for me, I'll shag you." Many of the photos and much of the text had been removed from the inside of the catalogue but its loss was more than amply compensated for with the addition of large quantities of hair, nail clippings and off-cuts of cloth taped into the pages.

There was a kind of home made rubber plant thing made of various raggedy pieces of green cloth. A ribbon wound round it read: "My umbrageous little sausage tree" and when Weed saw that he wanted to cry.

Practically every drawer contained an article or image of everyday life, a random phrase or word or some obscure arrangement of objects. It seemed to Weed that even the emptiness of some drawers was significant and that the contents of the others might be significant to only two people on the planet: he and whoever put them there.

When Weed had seen so much he needed to stop looking for a moment, he found that there was a multicoloured curtain of paper clips hanging across this alley between the filing cabinets: a partition or a doorway leading to another phase of the objects he had seen around him; or if those objects were thoughts, he might now be close to the kernel of the being that had thought them. Or it might conceal the entrance to the lavatory he was seeking. Weed pushed his way through.

He entered a square space that was walled with more of the same filing cabinets. The space was a good bedroom size and contained a bed — an unmade one — constructed of stacked reams of computer printout, cardboard, shredded paper and covered with a Snoopy-design quilt. There was an ample easy chair also made of stacked paper and a regular office desk and a computer terminal. The computer had been smothered in bright paper flowers and the screen filled with a mirror. Some cosmetics stood in an impatient crowd on the desk by the computer, furry slippers lay obediently by the bed. Draped over half-opened drawers was a compelling display of freshly laundered women's clothes. The place was clean but very much lived in.

Weed now needed to know what was in the file drawers here at the centre of this big imagination. He strode into the centre of the room and over to the bed. Choosing the drawer closest to the head of the bed, the locus of whatever dream this might be, he yanked it open. With an audible gasp of surprise he saw that the drawer was empty even of socks. Weed stared at the faintly grimy floor of the drawer and experimented with a couple of surprised gasps before deciding that the audible gasp of surprise that had accompanied the opening of the drawer had not been his own. He whirled around belatedly, but nonetheless dramatically and saw that a young woman had entered the room from the far side.

Weed's face cringed in guilt; cringed, cowered, curled up and crawled around trying to find a hole to hide in. The woman looked defiant but tearful. He waited for the demands to know on what authority he was prying here. He waited for the quietly measured contempt and well contained threats. He waited for the calls to Stonewall and to building security and to the police, for surely he was out of bounds and an obvious pervert hunting for the young female occupant's underwear drawer. There was no way he had not once again offended the very soul of Daikon AirCon with his wilful — or witless — inability to do anything right. Yes, that's what the woman's expression meant: bottomless disappointment and dismay at his unbounded capacity for incompetence.

'I suppose you've come for ...' sniffled this woman who had to be another Ms. Wap, a Wap clone. 'I'm ...' She consulted the nails on her right hand and then put them away in her left armpit where she might easily find them if she wanted to chew them later.

'I hope you realise that you forced me into this.' She knotted her arms over her chest and glared at the back of the computer.

So there it was, instant dismissal. Summary dismissal. Summary bullet-through-the-back-of-the-head dismissal. He joined the woman in glaring at the computer as if this shared task would forge some bond of sympathy between them.

It seemed not to work. 'Well, what are you going to do?' she asked in a tone that strongly suggested Weed ought to have done something.

'I suppose I'll begin with an apology — do want that in writing? Then I'll go by personnel and pick up my papers. Then, with everyone's permission, I'll be off.'

'Papers?' asked the woman, shocked. 'Have you been sacked?'

'Haven't I?' asked Weed.

'I don't know! It was you that said you were going to pick up your papers. What are you doing?'

Weed suddenly felt that he had suffered some kind of reversal but without any sense of having been on top he could not figure out why this might be.

'You said it was all my fault and I was just looking for the toilet ...'

'You were going to urinate in that drawer right by my bed, right by where I put my head at night?'

'Not literally,' said Weed tentatively.

'You were just pretending to urinate by my bed?'

'No. Not even that. I was looking for the toilet and I got distracted by the drawer right by where you put your head at night.' There Weed had said what he wanted to say. He waited for a thunderbolt and discovering himself to persist as Robert D. Weed and in no way resembling a lump of fulgurite, took the chance to elaborate a little.

'They said the toilet was over here. There.' Weed gestured in most directions at once without any clue from where he had been sent or to where. 'And I sort of found your drawer when I didn't know where I was.'

'You mean you're hopelessly lost in a maze of monstrously large filing cabinets!'

Weed was delighted to have somebody else put a name to it like that.

'Yes!'

'With a full bladder!'

'Yes!'

'Which, after wandering around here like Theseus without his ball of string for God knows how long, must be excruciatingly painful!'

'Yes!' exclaimed Weed. Nobody had ever shown him such understanding before. He thought he might fall in love out of simple gratitude.

'Come with me,' said the woman and darted out the room. Without the merest trace of a puzzled pause, Weed was off after her.

She led him at a rapid, authoritative pace through more maze and then some more maze until they came to a corner of the building where there was a men's toilet and a women's toilet.

A sort of his and hers arrangement, thought Weed, and wondered jealously where the other man might be.

'I never go in there,' said his guide pointing at the men's. 'I expect it's a bit of a mess.'

Weed stepped in and turned the light on.

Evidently this corner of this floor of this building was a forgotten land, a place lost beyond the maze of filing cabinets. Nobody came here.

The men's room looked like a twee little winter wonderland. The hidden strip lighting showed Weed a little world cloaked in white powder — not grey like usual dust, but soft, snowy white. Paper dust perhaps, from all those busy printing machines churning out ton upon ton of numbers everyday; numbers flaked into dust and floated in here where nobody ever cleaned up. Here the numbers rest in peace in their own fluffy heaven. As he walked he left footprints on the floor but he tried very hard to disturb as little of the magical dust as possible.

The woman was waiting outside the toilet, arms knotted again. She was a tad on the short side, wore her black hair in a bob that was not exactly a bob, and she had dark but not soft eyes.

She said as Weed emerged 'I'm sorry I mistook you for something else. Would you like a cup of tea?'

Weed sure would, and much later the unsteady rattle of his sixth mug of tea as he put it down on the computer table told him eloquently that he was in love. Her name was Bobette Hope and she was obviously beautiful both inside and out; and Weed had no reason to believe that the bits in between weren't similarly sublime. Or he might just be trembling from too much tannin and caffeine.

It seemed that Weed's bursting bladder had dispelled Bobette's mistrust and the initial offer of a cuppa had replicated itself half a dozen times, enough to fill the entire afternoon.

They talked; they both talked, and they did not just take it in turns to present monologues which is the way a lot of conversations go these days. They talked about whatever it was the other had just said, and asked each other questions to learn more about what they thought. Conversations with his employers, their avatars, or his fellow trainees had never yielded a degree of reciprocity; conversations with his parents had never bothered with give and take. Talking to Warren had approximated this attention and response, but this was much better. This was Nirvana compared to Luton. For a start, Bobette was a great deal better looking than Warren. No offence, Warren. Then she was a lot better informed about the sorts of things that Weed specially liked, and, mostly, her sense of humour was consistently comprehensible. And through the afternoon they learned something about each other and they expressed honest feelings about things, which was something Weed was not able to do very often and which felt very, very good. It was as if Bobette had opened his curtains and opened his windows to let sunlight and some nice fresh air into him, and was inspiring him to do a little dusting about the place to boot.

'Did you put all those things in those drawers?' Weed asked.

'Yes,' said Bobette flushing. 'It, er ...'

'They're quite funny,' Weed reassured her. 'Funny and whimsical ... and quite meaningful in a totally obscure kind of way. They made me feel very curious.'

'I was just trying to brighten up the place a bit,' Bobette explained. 'I haven't had too much to do lately. Besides, the drawers were begging for it. They remind me very much of racked skulls. Heads, really. Not dead or anything morbid like that. Just sort of stacked or packed. Like commuters on a train, or workers in a high rise office building, or the residents of one of those big blocks of flats

— like that disgusting Heavenly Estate in the north of the city. And they seemed kind of vacant ... potential.'

Weed knew exactly what she meant.

'The label holder on each drawer is like a little "Oh!" of surprise or dismay on a blank face. I'm never sure whether they're having the time of their lives or just plain drowning,' he said.

'And you, erm ...' Weed observed, indicating the bed and the furniture and the generally lived-in aura of the room.

'Yes, I live here,' she admitted. 'Have done for quite some time now.'

'If you're not so busy?'

'I was hired as a temp. A data entry job, they told me. Could turn permanent, they suggested.' Bobette was curled on the bed. She looked very comfortable like a character in a coffee commercial — except they were drinking tea and neither of them liked coffee. Her face was very far away as if recounting events from a very different life.

'They wanted to digitise all these old records. All these filing cabinets in this labyrinth were stuffed full of paper records back then. Been sitting around various Daikon offices for yonks. From before computers, of course. I don't know why they couldn't just bin them. Brought them all here.' She yawned. 'I retyped them on the computer terminal. Shredded the originals. Pressed a key on the keyboard which transferred the data to another computer elsewhere.'

'Wow!' said Weed. 'How many of you were there?'

Bobette raised concerned eyebrows at Weed. 'Just me, she said, as if it were self evident. 'My supervisor gave me six months to finish and walked out of here. I haven't seen her since. Which is just as well. She was a real cow as I remember.'

'You were expected to do all that yourself?' Weed was incredulous.

'Well, it was my first job of this kind. It was my first job not dishing slop in a fast-crap restaurant. What did I know?'

'What happened?'

'I drove myself half potty trying to meet the deadline. I wanted that permanent job I thought they had going. I wanted it really badly. There are so few jobs around that actually pay. And I kind of thought there would be some security with Daikon AirCon. Hell! I imagined a permanent post and instant promotion if I got this finished in time. I thought they'd be so impressed. I found that I was spending so much time in here keeping on top of the deadline I figured I may as well just move in here.

'I like to do a good job, but I think I became a little obsessed, worked just about twenty hours a day, weekends too, on the whole. Seems odd looking back on it.'

'So you missed the deadline and you're in the doghouse.'

Bobette looked affronted. 'No way! At the stroke of midnight on the final day I pressed that little send key for the final time, sent a message I had finished and fell asleep for a couple of days. Well, to cut a long story short, nobody got back to me. I went home but found my flat had been re-let. But the funny thing is, I didn't care. I no longer felt I belonged in the outside world. Nobody knew or cared what I had just done, and when I tried to tell my friends or family they just glazed over and started talking about themselves. I felt like an alien in my own environment. And everything seemed so trite and shallow and pointless. Getting married and having kids or reading poems or sending people to Mars all just seemed to be missing the point. The point being, there was printed information to be digitised.

'I started collecting bits and pieces and bringing it back here. During my regular working hours I'd put it on the computer. And I could not resist hitting that little send button. Somewhere in Daikon's computers there are several gigabytes of advertising leaflets, bus tickets, till receipts, comics, raffle tickets, food wrappers — you name it I put it in there.

'I suppose I wasn't too far gone because I went to see a doctor eventually. He said I had PMTSD — Post Mindless Task Stress Disorder. The only cure apparently is a well-paid job where you get to exercise your intelligence and initiative. He gave me a prescription for one, but the chemist said he'd taken the last good job himself and there were no more available anywhere for the likes of me.'

'So here you are,' said Weed, somewhat overawed by the afternoon and everything in it. 'And what is Daikon doing with you now?'

'Nothing. That's another funny thing. Everyday I send them a message to say I've finished and nothing and no one comes back. They pay me like clockwork. I do nothing. It's like I've fallen through a crack in their system. I hate to do nothing while they're paying me still, but if they will ignore my messages, that has to be their fault in the end, doesn't it?'

'In the meantime you decorate drawers.'

'And avoid the real world. At least I've cured myself of putting everything I see onto their computer. Though I have to admit to having prettified the inside of it with some poems from Rumi and Rilke and so on. I couldn't resist.' From mischievous she suddenly looked tearful.

'I'd love to go back to how it was before. But I can't. There's nothing out there, nobody, to anchor me. I don't know how to deal with it. My life is here now.'

By the time Weed staggered out of the grey labyrinth, tipsy with tannin and drunk on caffeine, he had decided to make it his project to be that anchor in the real world that Bobette needed.

In his euphoria it failed to cross his mind that he had missed an entire afternoon's sales workshop. It was a shame because he would have enjoyed it. It was entitled *Discovering advanced sales techniques, Core 6*. The blurb in the manual went "suppose all the penguins at the North Pole could talk. Develop a sales strategy to deploy in a one-to-one contact scenario in the frozen North. How would you convince a penguin it lacked an air conditioner? Don't melt too much ice with those warm smiles! Global warming caused by unnecessary and irresponsible energy consumption is already seeing to that — so be sure to turn off the lights in the seminar centre when you leave! This is a problem we at Daikon AirCon have long been combating by fitting inverters to all installations of over 100W! When you have finished your discussion and presentation our experienced sales technicians will tell you how you should have done it."

On reading this the day before, Weed had joked to Ms. Wap, 'This is going to be a terribly short seminar — there are no penguins in the Arctic. They all live in the southern hemisphere.'

'Do shut up, Bob,' said Ms. Wap sweetly. 'Who ever heard of penguins in Africa?'

The next morning Weed shot out of bed as if Bobette herself was waiting with Ms. Wap at the training centre — the Prerequisites Acquisition Locus, to give it its correct name, or our PAL, the Womb, or Boot Camp as it was also known to the higher-ups and old hands. Of course, Bobette was nowhere near the Prerequisites Acquisition Locus. She was in section HUG/1, which was located adjacent to the Human Resources Project in Adam Smith House near the centre of the city, more than several miles from where Weed was going.

And what going it was! It takes Weed an hour and a half to get there from the Heavenly Estate because Daikon would never want an address even in the same hemisphere of the city as a part of town as shoddy as that. That is one and a half hours if the transport system was running right. In reality Weed had to leave two hours for the journey to compensate for diverted trains and derailed buses, the action of terrorists, snow or sunlight. Even then he was late pathetically often.

What normally bothered him most was that the other trainees were never late. They all rolled in a respectable ten minutes ahead of start time, fresh and vigorous even though many of them had further to travel than Weed. They would be full of the tales of the morning's transport atrocities, how their train went in the wrong direction and was stranded for forty minutes in a siding in an undiscovered part of town where roam dinosaurs, of how a demonstration against public protests had brought the entire city to a standstill with marchers laying in the road in every major thoroughfare. It seemed that on every occasion the trainees had mysteriously predicted the disruption and had allowed that much extra journey time to compensate for it or avoid it altogether. It made Weed look very bad indeed when he stumbled in twenty minutes late and rank with sweat despite the subzero temperatures.

Why didn't his colleagues do something useful with this gift of clairvoyance, Weed wondered, like winning the lottery or predicting earthquakes, instead of merely using it to navigate this dreary routine?

Today, as Weed made his way to the station his thoughts were entirely of Bobette — he was buoyed by his new-found project. He was now invincible, inured: he wore the shiny armour of one who has a future. Today he was untouchable, he was ready for Daikon AirCon and Ms. Wap; he could take anything they could throw at him. Today their arrows and barbs would bounce off his armour. He was in love.

However, love had not yet afflicted the rail system and the trains were too crowded to physically get on. The train guards had recently been fired en masse and only freelances were being used. These freelance train guards were in fact the same people who had just been fired, and who had been rehired on a different contract. Now they were only paid when the train was standing at a station and they were doing something other than staring out the window at the hurtling cows. When they were between stations, the company argued, the guards were doing nothing useful and were therefore just dead weight. There had been some protest, but the company had pointed out that rail travel was expensive and that on a long run from one end of the country to the other, the regular fare exceeded what the guard was actually paid, so the rail company was actually being very generous to allow him to stay on the train for that time.

In the spirit of the new responsibilities that came with the guards' self employed status, a productivity bonus system was arranged, whereby guards were paid extra in proportion to excess of projected passenger load for that day and that time of day.

The result was guards were holding the train up as long as possible at each station to maximise their earnings. They would wait until no other people could physically fit on the train before reluctantly closing the doors and allowing the following train, stalled just up the track with its sweaty, asphyxiating, compressed cargo to enter the station.

After the third aborted connection Weed had solved the problem by crawling on to the train between people's legs. This had provoked a lot of kicking and stomping and near suffocation but had done the trick in the long run. Once at work, he was shoved into a van and driven across town back to the Heavenly Estate, his original point of departure.

With his day's assignment he was on his way through the Nirvana Heights underpass on his way to Elysium Fields Tower when he was stopped by three young men. When they discovered that the smartly dressed, if malodorous, Weed was carrying half a pack of cigs and only enough money for a cursory lunch, they beat him up and stole his shoes.

By now, Yard's agile bulk had propelled itself as far as the tenth floor where it paused to refill its fast emptying weapon, mop sweat and ease the stitch in its side. As the motion-provoked swaying of his loose, blubbery mantle ceased, he became aware of another vibration, asynchronous with his familiar own, that was low and insistent, and which penetrated to Yard's remote core where it inspired a faint nausea before being finally absorbed. It was a sensation not dissimilar to hunger except that it began at his feet and worked its way up.

He waded obliviously through a family exiting by the fire doors and entered the body of the building. There the vibration, accompanied by a low chthonian rumble, engulfed him. Down the long blank corridor to the fire doors at the lift well the strip lighting flickered incontinently. He inflated himself to his full height and girth, adopted a smile like a banana split and, gurgling happily, proceeded.

In the erratic light Yard could make out a dark huddled mass halfway down toward the lifts. He drew the bolt on his Uzi and held it out ahead of him one handed. In his paw the thing looked little more than a toy. The black pile heaved and flopped still. It had now resolved itself into a mess of tentacles spilling across the hall from a doorway as if some giant squid were trying to free itself from the tiny flat.

A loud clanging startles Yard. It comes from the steel door immediately to his right and he has to check the impulse to fire, leery of ricochets. The banging becomes louder, more urgent, then the door bursts from its frame and Yard is immediately smothered by a tonne of writhing roots.

He rolls onto his front and heaves, comes up from the vegetable depths swinging his blade to loosen the last intimate holds of this presumptuous plant. Once upright, he remains thigh deep in the tangle. In front of him dozens of slatted, head-sized leaves on craning stalks bob and sway, bewildered to find themselves there, wondering what they are doing so close to their roots. Yard licks some of the ice cream off his banana-split smile and readies his blade about his ear — which is about as high as he can raise his arm — and picks out with relish the arc of his first swing. The motion of the leaves changes abruptly to a frenzied thrashing so that the doorway and the leaves appear to Yard as the maw and poisonous incisors on an enraged jabberwocky.

Beyond them, the creature's black heart is forcing its way up the gullet, thickly wrapped in viscera, to personally oversee the policeman's dismemberment. Yard let it have it long and good, firing from his outstretched arm, whose heavy trunk easily absorbed the weapon's buck. Something inside the flat recoiled.

'Ha!' thinks Yard — then the doorway copiously vomits plant stuff. Embedded in the crest of the spume is a grotesque mannequin, flapping loosely as it is shoved in Yard's face for his inspection — for it is his own work. Yard bats it away in disgust with a big boxing-glove fist and it flops onto the convoluted versant of the root pile. It is the formerly missing Mr. Perkins who is just about the former Mr. Perkins, twitching violently and expiring with a long gurgle and riddled with Yard's bullets.

'You have the right to remain silent,' Yard began. 'You are entitled to, er ... something, and one phone call, and, er ... a cup of tea, but not a very good one.' Yard knew he was obliged to read the arrested their rights, but could never remember what they were. 'Ok, Perkins, you're nicked. Obstruction — to wit, obstructing the progress of police bullets, you twit — endangerment, assaulting a pi — a police officer, constipation — I mean conspiracy — and bleeding on the carpet. You are going to come quietly. It is a well known scientific fact that cooperating with the authorities vastly reduces your chances of falling down stairs.'

Yard observes with a professional eye that the almost late inhabitant of number 1,249 Nirvana Heights is uniformly covered with a fine white dust which nicely shows up the bright whorish smear of blood round his mouth, and that his hair and pyjamas contain lumps of plaster and masonry. Perkins must have been displaced from his bed, carried down through two floors and laterally through several walls before being regurgitated through the doorway of number 1,064 here and into the path of Yard's bullets. And all while the poor git was still in his jimjams. Yard might have wondered what kind of monster it was that was filling up the interior of Nirvana heights with greenery, but he thinks he already knows.

However, knowing is not helping right now. Yard is trapped, pinned against the wall, chest deep in the spillage over which newly arrived tentacles slither. Out of sight, hirsute fingers probe his nethers, perhaps assessing his nutritional value, his nitrogen content. Encased, Yard wobbles helplessly. The floor sags, tearing away from the skirting with a muffled whump that expels fat billows of dust through the crevices and pores of the tangled vegetable.

Fighting to regain his footing he cackles into his radio, 'A real party, up here. Room for a few more if you've nothing better to do.' This is the closest he has ever come to saying he needed help — this is possibly the first time he has needed help and the phenomenon amuses him.

'Time!' exclaims Yard, as if he has an urgent appointment at his grandmother's. 'Time to make like a tree and leave.' With an endearing burble of delight he swells and gathers himself tightly into a yet rounder shape and moves, urging his gargantuan bulk against the tons of tangled creeper. He barges belly-first and the root pack moves minutely with him until the floor beneath exhales once more, spilling another knotty tsunami downhill at his head. Up to his nose in it now, Yard puts his shoulder down and his adversary retreats in a slow skid, still tenaciously braced against him.

'Oh? Sumo salad, is it?' asks Yard. The reluctant theatre judders around them and Yard slips out of sight beneath the coils.

It was a shell — a hollow, grey and cracked shell. Whatever had incubated here had long since vacated, abandoned the place, given it up, evacuated and fled.

'Just right. Just right for our modest purposes — or immodest ones if you get lucky, eh, Bob?' said his dad. 'A place to kick off. A place to meet someone, get married. Have kids. First foot on the ladder. Though I wouldn't leap into it, you know. Nothing like being young with your whole future laid out before you. Look around a bit. See what's on the supermarket shelves before you buy. Know what I mean? But apart from that, a lovely place to kick off.'

They were in Weed's flat — but before it was Weed's flat. They were there — Weed's dad was there — with a view to buy. With Weed's money. With money Weed had yet to earn.

Weed senior was very impressed with his son's salary. He had never in his life earned anything like it. In fact he had spent most of his life not earning anything. Weed junior might have been impressed with his salary if he was earning anything like the salary Weed senior thought he was earning, however, the salary projections set out in the recruitment blurb did not remotely match the reality of his pay cheques. Obviously the projection in the blurb was taken on the earnings of an experienced and dynamic individual working an upmarket area of Riyadh on a particularly hot day. Weed was a useless salesman working some of the most deprived neighbourhoods in a country where the sun was a semi mythical object.

'It'll appreciate like billio, like a lucky lottery ticket. Fifteen, twenty years, move up to a little house, a maisonette. You'll be in a semi before you know it!'

'Dad — '

'Just the place to assert your new found status: a young professional! A man of independent means needs a lifestyle to match. You can do things here. Have your mates round or whatever your fancy ... ' He winked at his son.

'Dad —'

Weed's dad was not a big man, he was the sort you could lose in a shag pile. But he did not carry himself like a small man. Every movement was full of assertion. He squared up to anything that could suggest he lacked stature. He squared up to tables, chairs and dingy derelict flats.

'It's lovely, Robert,' said Weed's mum.

'Mum —'

'We'll be sorry to see you move out of course — even though it will give us a sitting room. But we're not going to stand in your way, love.'

'That's right,' said Mr. Weed, hands clasped behind his back and striding assertively around the lightless cubicle that was to be Weed's new home.

'You got chances, Bob. Chances I only ever wanked about. Not even that, 'cos I didn't even think in them days that chances like yours ever existed. You got a good job, a job with prospects. In your short years you already done more than I done at your age. Mind you I done a bit since, but that's my age.

When I went out to work there weren't no such things as opportunities. All they wanted then was men to go down the sewers. So down the drains I went, and all the rest of us. But you're doing good son. And I like to think I gave you a leg up — not blowing my own horn. Tried to give yer a push in the right direction, give yer something I never had. And that's what I'm doing now. Giving yer another leg up, settling yer down in this gaff. It may look cruel but you'll thank my ferret.'

'One thing, John,' said Mrs. Weed, frozen in mid thought. 'Are you sure we approve?'

Mr. Weed stepped sideways across the room with a motion that would have been a rapid and purposeful stride in a larger space, but was an arthritic shuffle in this one.

He squared off with Mrs. Weed somewhere around her midriff.

'What's that, love?' he asked in a tone that very much suggested he disapproved of the possibility that there may be something to disapprove of.

''E's a adult, inne?'

'Yes, but,' said Mrs. Weed collecting words from the cloud of them in the air around her head as quickly as possible and finding an order for them. 'This building and all the others around, they was built with taxpayers' money and given to people without much of their own and they was a triffic help though they are ugly as sin and a refuge for hardened criminals and I wouldn't wish one on a dog, having lived in one such for so many years. Then the government said the tenants could buy them even though there still wasn't enough places to go round. And you called the government evil scum-sucking bastards, thieving from the poor to give to their own. Then the tenants what bought the places at knockdown prices started selling the flats again for knock-up prices and you called them evil scum-sucking bastards too. Now you're trying to get our Robert to buy one.'

Weed was glad his mum had pointed this out. It was just what he had been thinking.

Mr. Weed was silent a moment, waiting for his wife to come out of her cloud of words and look down at him.

'Dad, I—' said Weed.

'Never let it be said,' said Mr. Weed, now he had his wife's full, renewed attention. 'Never let it be said that I don't admit my own mistakes.' He shook his head solemnly and waved a hand to pre-emptively ward off any attempts to stop him admitting his own mistakes.

'I did say that, it's true. And I meant it at the time. But I was wrong.' He strolled off to find a wall to confess to. 'I was taking the short view, wasn't I; I wasn't taking the long view.' He surfed a hand through the air to suggest length or on-goingness.

'I wasn't looking ahead.'

And now Weed thought about it, he realised that they weren't selling the flats in the Weeds' block.

'Now I see what a marvellous opportunity for ordinary folk the sell-off was. Quite brilliant.' He turned round to make sure his family didn't miss the full broadside of his enlightenment.

'You own your own home, you're your own little king in it. King! It frees people from slavery to the state, a state that would like to dictate to us from cradle to grave, which mollycoddles us and wraps us in cocoons of security till we don't know how to look after ourselves no more. It robs us of initiative and ... and ... the other thing ... the dignity what comes of being fully in control of our own density.

'Owning things, now, owning things comes with responsibility. Or is it the other way round? Anyway, we have responsibility for the things we own for a start. Responsibility for decisions we make by ourselves.' Mr. Weed was now threatening the grey air with his fist.

'The responsibility of, of ... self-automation. It builds character. It's ... character building. It learns yer to stand on yer own two feet. In yer own gaff nobody, but nobody, can tell yer what to do.

'We been renting since we got married. And what have we got now? Nuffin except a disability allowance.'

Mr. Weed stood his ground and shook his fist at the molecules of dinge until he realised he had finished.

He summed up: 'When yer owns fings, yer a little king.'

There was a short and respectful silence, and then Weed said, 'B —' and his mother said, 'Well, all right then, John, if you're sure we don't disapprove. Now what about ... things — stuff?'

They all paused to stare reflectively at the four walls, the floor and the ceiling. Apart from the sink and the kitchen cabinets, whose plastic laminate coating was split and curling and whose layers were avoiding each other as if afraid of some horrific contagion, the place already had some stuff: stuff that was growing on the wallpaper and the skirting board, stuff that lurked in the disintegrating carpet underlay, stuff that had died or been murdered by other stuff, and stuff that cowered in damp rimes of despair and terror in the corners.

'You'll need to make time to redecorate, of course,' Weed was told.

Time? Weed didn't have time to wipe his own bottom these days, when was he going to have time to redecorate?

'And you'll need a cooker and a fridge ...'

'A tv of course, a stereo for the young exec ...'

'Pots, pans, cups, glasses, knives, forks ...'

'A nice table and a comfy sofa ...'

'A bed, wardrobe, bath towels and mat ...'

'Cat ...'

'Shelves to put all his books on ...'

'Microwave oven ...'

'Three-speed rotisserie ...'

'A compact integrated automatic washing machine and tumble drier ...'

'Blender and liquidiser with accessories and attachments ...'

'Coffee percolator with fully computerised timer function and built-in alarm ...'

'Automatic tea maker with built-in digital flat-screen tv ...'

'Serving trolley with hot plates and fully swivelling wheels ...'

'A set of authentic Staffordshire bone china ...'

'Lawn mower, wheel barrow, and eight-speed hedge trimmer ...'

'Cuddly toy ...'

'A big cheese plant ...'

Weed's folks lapsed into awed silence. Everything they had never had but had seen on tv, all the trappings of full membership of the human race would go to their son.

Eventually Weed said, 'Erm —' and his father stilling him with another of his vast repertoire of open-handed gestures said 'I know what you're thinking, Robert. You're thinking you need a way to thank me for all this, for seeing the agent and the bank on your behalf. Well there's no need, believe me. What are fathers for? You're the busy little exec now. Just think of me as your manager, your agent, your coach, your personal assistant. Only too glad to help.'

Actually Weed was thinking buying now was rushing into things a little bit. He hadn't actually started earning the money yet. And the flat was a God-awful little hole. Why not skip this first rung on the property ladder and go straight on to the next stage — a soggy cardboard box, for example?

'Still nothing.'

'Better find him quick. Won't be able to move up here soon.'

'We will find him,' asserts Captain Flack who is in charge of the Executive Action Group sent up into Nirvana Heights to find Inspector Yard.

'Pugh, Pugh, Barney MacGrew: try the next floor if you can. Cuthbert, cover the stairs. Dibble, Grubb — with me. We're going to see what's the other side of that pile of crap. But careful! The floor looks a bit dodgy.'

The group moves up, covering each other with their big rifles, covering the still, black pile, covering the shadows, as if they are performing a slow macho ballet, or as if they are on tv.

'What's that?'
'What?'
'It moved!'
'It didn't!'
'It bloody did!'
'What moved?'
'That black thing.'
'Get off!'

'Look! It did it again!'

'Nah!'

'No, he's right, it did move!'

'There, see?'

'You been doing too much steroids, that's what — bleeding hell! Down everybody!'

'Bloody told you!'

'Down, I said! All right, everybody, keep calm. Don't shoot until you see the white of its stamen.'

In the trembling hollow of the tower, under the madly fulgurating lights, the big flop of plant heaves and lurches. Its flank swells and rises, sways and tumbles toward them.

'Hold your fire! Hold your fire! Get ready —'

It rises once more — if a rubber plant had rear legs and was inclined to rear threateningly, this is how it would look. The whole thing shakes with an uncontrollable inner fury and bursts, birthing Swamp Thing itself with a loud splat, the impact nearly deciding the un-shored floor.

Captain Flack is too busy dangling his jaw to give the order to fire.

The Swamp Thing monster, huge beyond good sense and all writhing roots and branches and coal red eyes, flounders forward on all fours straining to break its last umbilical ties. It rights itself via its knees and with a triumphant flex of its shoulders is free. The floor gives way in a bellow of white dust that, like Hell reclaiming its spawn, consumes the Swamp Thing thing before smothering the gob-smacked cops.

When the Executive Action Group has vented its shock in spluttering and gagging and the air has cleared enough to reveal the absence of walls and floor where the giant pile of roots had been, they turn to their escape and freeze. There behind them is the green monster, straddling the space between them and the stairs. It is wearing Yard's head and even speaks with Yard's voice.

'Any of you lot know what a rhizome is? Ok, you see anything you don't recognise, shoot it.' Yard seems happy at this and, pulling the last skeins of root from his shoulders, heads for the stairs, suddenly less like Swamp Thing and more like the Jolly Green Giant and singing 'Tiptoe Through the Tulips'.

At last Flack remembers to give the fire order. Pulling a battered pack of cigarettes from his pocket, he says 'Light me!'

Behind Heavenly Estate, a strange, greenish aurora wriggled in the sky. Sergeant Testosteroni is standing on top of his APC, arms akimbo, binoculars hanging on his chest. This is just how Rommel would have looked surveying Tobruk in 1942, if Tobruk had looked like a well tossed salad and if Rommel had sported a dangly beer gut and had possessed a face like a sausage breakfast.

In the unstill and lurid light, the good sergeant can see that Nirvana Heights has coyly cloaked its naked concrete in big leaves. Foliage hangs in thick bunches from the windows contentedly chattering with the light breeze and the sun. Creepers play snakes and ladders up and down its sheer face, and a larval flow of roots has burst from the lower windows, the entrances and the underpass, and lays like a fidgety Hawaiian skirt around the tower's base.

It is the most sinister thing Testosteroni has ever seen. It is entirely green — and isn't that bloke in Nightmare on Elm Street green? He wonders about its origins — whether it is of a good family, which it can't be that colour, or any colour that is different from the sergeant's own — and about its import. But he isn't worried. It is just a plant, and moreover, a contained plant. The combined constabularies of the city's northern sector are drawn up, under helmets and behind shields, in a thick blue line around the building. Behind the police cordon are the massed operatives of the city's Directorate of Parks and Benches, whose initial black-eyed belligerence at being hoicked out of bed so unnatural that even their watches failed to register it, had become wide-eyed in wonder when confronted with so much easy pruning to be done on double time. They now leaned expertly on their shovels and scythes and gestured authoritatively at the plant. When they have all finished their well-urned tea they will move in.

The evacuation of the neighbouring building blocks had gone well, with only a hundred and sixteen injured in the stampede. The evacuees were now sheltering in the nearby schools and community halls, the residents of Nirvana Heights having a primary school all to themselves where they were being methodically debriefed and questioned about the whereabouts and activities in the last twenty-four hours of any leftover salad that may have contained GM ingredients, and whether they had any friends or relatives with unusually green fingers.

A headcount was made. Several people including Inspector Yard, Captain Flack's Executive Action Group, Mr. Perkins, Robert D. Weed and Warren were unaccounted for.

Air conditioners, in case you don't know, are wonderful machines that help to facilitate efficient and orderly breathing. The air we breathe has been inhaled and exhaled by all the other people around you — and if you happen to be standing outside and there is a stiff breeze blowing, the air you are breathing may have travelled all round the world and may have been already breathed by people as far away as China or Wales. Imagine that!

The humble air you are pushing in and out of your nose has probably swept across the Steppes or maybe even Patagonia; it may have slalomed through the arches of the Coliseum, or played tag among the foliage of the Hanging Gardens of Babylon. Have you been to these places? I know I haven't. Lucky old air! And then, on its way from, say, Bangkok to, say, Tasmania, it's stops by your alveoli to keep you alive a while longer. Lucky us! Busy old air!

While the air is rushing about it gets all mixed up. It gets mixed up with itself, and if trapped inside buildings, it gets mixed up with the steamy gases we exhale and the garlicky, tobaccoey, boozy, belchy, farty fumes that we exude as a natural result of leading fun lives, and gets all mixed up with the ozone from our appliances, cigarette smoke, dioxin, sulphur dioxide and the black diesel particles that are also a result of us leading fun lives.

Indoors, the air just hangs about getting stale and bored and all the more mixed up, and for us it's like breathing some kind of musty, dank treacle. The air would like to go outside and freshen itself up by giving its yucky bits to a tree or some other natural filter, and perhaps reinvigorate itself with a quick zoom to Alaska or New Zealand, but it cannot because the window is shut or there aren't any windows or because we have an air conditioner. Let's face it, it would be a shame not to use the damned machine after going to all the trouble and expense of having it invented and then buying it. Many modern buildings, particularly offices, are designed to take full advantage of this little technological wonder. They take advantage by not having openable windows. A building with un-openable windows has two great strengths. One is that people have to use the doors to get in and out. This makes people flow management easier and keeps the pavements outside less cluttered with splatted body parts. Second, the air conditioning system can work its magic without pollution from any unruly and unconditioned air that might get in from outside.

You see, the air conditioner works by hoovering up the steamy, confused, higgledy-piggledy air and rearranging all its molecules in straight, buffed lines. The longer the air remains inside, the straighter and more regimented the lines of molecules become. This is what we call micro-management. The process renders the air in a condition where it is able to slip down our tracheas without undue friction or congestion. Breathing becomes easier. Happily, this has a positive knock-on in industrial productivity because the less attention and energy a worker expends on breathing, the more thorough and efficient will be the work.

This is not the only way the air conditioner helps to keep the wheels of industry spinning.

Firstly, air conditioners have to be made, which fills up people's time screwing the components together. This activity provides the screwing operatives with just enough salary to buy for their own homes one of the air conditioners they just made. Air conditioners are not cheap: buying an air conditioner is not like buying a packet of crisps. The screwing operative might want to pay in instalments on a SupaLayAway HP plan, where you pay back just two percent of the total purchase price per month over several years so you hardly notice it. This is arranged by your local building society at fifteen percent per annum, which helps to fill up the days of yet more people filling out forms and operating the computers which calculate the interest on your behalf, and in turn provides these lucky people with enough salary to buy themselves an air conditioner and avail themselves of the service they administer. Moreover, the air conditioner is composed of materials which have to be mined and processed and it runs on electricity which also has to be mined and then assembled from plutonium atoms in a reactor. All this mining activity, as with manufacturing and hire-purchasing, keeps a lot of people busy inside when they might otherwise be making things for themselves which would never find their way into the global marketplace, or they would be cluttering up the countryside with bicycles and tents. This process also liberates a lot of minerals, which would otherwise be unproductively taking up valuable space in the Earth's mantle. The mining also thoughtfully liberates future generations from the labour of extracting the minerals themselves because we will have used them all. This will ultimately boost labour efficiency by leaving future generations with their hands free to combat global warming, which is a result of manufacturing and running such fun gadgets as air conditioners.

Let us not underestimate the environmental impact of air conditioners. We do not need to take a purely utilitarian view to these machines. There is a fuzzier side to them as well.

Around the world natural habitats are being productively altered, and many species are under pressure to adapt to the demands of modern living or die out. Air conditioners, however, are presenting new ecosystems to those creatures that are ready to use their Darwinian skills to adapt. The temperature and humidity in air conditioners make them excellent breeding conditions for all kinds of life. All kinds of viruses have made the evolutionary leap and taken advantage of the protected stable environment that air conditioners offer. When will elephants and tigers and cod make the same leap? Well, that's up to them, isn't it.

In this way, while the biosphere is under tremendous pressure from mining, CO_2 emissions from tired loan clerks, electricity generation to power air conditioners, and so on, Daikon AirCon is doing its bit to succour biological life. And, make no mistake, this is not the only action Daikon AirCon takes in protecting the environment in which we live. The company funds at least one environmental study group which reports back regularly that Daikon AirCon is having no negative impact on the environment at all. Three cheers for Daikon AirCon! And then, of course there are those plans to air condition the entire planet. The idea is to have massive air conditioners installed at locations so desolate no one will miss the space, such as the Sahara desert, both poles and the Heavenly Estate where Weed lives. Some ungracious individuals have pointed out that when air conditioners produce cold air, they produce and equal and opposite quantity of hot air from their backsides. No problem.

Daikon are going to build giant chimneys to deposit the hot air in outer space, which is absolutely freezing anyway. But what about all the extra energy the air conditioners will burn? Won't that … No! Shut up! It won't! Not even a little bit! So that's all right then. And anyway, when we have the planet fully environmentally controlled, Daikon AirCon will have complete control over everything and everyone and everything will be just the way Daikon AirCon likes it, and everyone will have to be the way Daikon AirCon wants them to be. Hail to Daikon AirCon!

And what of the future? Well, Daikon AirCon's research and development boffins are already looking at doing for light what air conditioners are doing for air. Think of the boost in workplace efficiency if we had light conditioners that removed the grey or brown that gets mixed up with the light so often then arrange all the photons in straight lines to slip more easily into the eye. With bright and glittery light, those workaday blues that sometimes afflict us would simply vanish!

So you can see that air conditioners are a wonderful boon especially if you live or work in a building that was designed without breathing in mind. But air conditioners aren't just for the huge places, as Ms. Wap would go to great pains to point out, an air conditioner will bring respiratory order and reassurance to the smallest and most humble abodes.

'You know what I'd be like?' asked Warren, who adored from afar Sharon in Procurements. 'I'd get me teeth into them and shake them till their back was broke.' Warren was in Weed's living room, in his shell suit, arms akimbo, legs akimbo, hair, teeth and nose akimbo. Weed was in the kitchenette which meant he was also in the living room. He was the opposite of akimbo, all wrapped around himself and a nice mug of tea.

'Like a dog with a rat. You seen them jock russels, them engineered hybrids of wolf hounds and jack russels out of that place in Scotland what made them radioactive sheep, or whatever, you seen how they get hold of rats and cats and that?

'You seen them ratting dogs, they get their teeth in and they shake and they don't let go for nothing. You can kick 'em bawl at them, hit them with a brat — a bat — and they just go on shaking until the little bleeder's back is broke. Cower a bit if you kick them but they won't let go, just kinda turn their back on you, maybe look at you as if you have no right there and maybe snarl a bit. Through their nose, they snarl, but they do it from their throat — right down. Dead creepy. Sinister. Totally evil.

'But they won't let go, not for nothing, cause it's theirs, you see. It's their thing and nobody's going to take it from them. It's competition. They got it, they got the rat by their best efforts in their minds, 'cos what do they know about domesticated and supermarkets, eh? That Filiigree Chump or whatever, as far as they're concerned, that's just gravy. That's from out of the blue — manna, like. They don't know Insanesbury's is packed with the stuff. As far as they're concerned this might be the only can in creation, an aberration of nature; rat accidentally born pre-chopped and ready to eat. So they cling on to what they got when they got it. Because that's survival to them, innit. Apart from which, it's hereditary.

'Anyway, it's totally animal.'

Weed concurred. He had seen such things. In his flat he had seen such events in the mould on the skirting board without the presence of ratting dogs.

'That's what I'd be like if I was a salesman. But I got GCSE Maths and English. That's what did for me. They put me in admin.'

Weed suffered the involuntary image of Warren savaging his admin colleagues with his teeth and shaking them until their backs were broken if they didn't get their form-filling procedures right.

Warren unlimbered from akimbo and fetched some tea to his mouth. He did not normally drink anything weaker than napalm spiked with vodka, but tea was all Weed had that night.

'Just see if I wasn't.'

Warren had materialised out of the blue or the grey at Weed's front door this evening. After months of living in the same building and working for the same company and travelling the same trains and buses, they had got together in the same room to have a chat and compare notes. Although quite in awe of Warren, who was the more assertive and outspoken being, Weed did a rare and bold thing: he spoke his mind.

'I don't actually like being a salesman. In fact, I hate it.'

It was not a rare thing that he wanted to speak his mind, nor was he reticent. This was the first time in months — or years — that he had been allowed to finish a sentence. He suddenly liked Warren. And he liked Warren even more when he appeared to take the time to think about what Weed had said. And in that time Weed was able to enlarge upon his theme.

'And I'm very, very crap at it. Unbelievably, mind bogglingly, staggeringly, shamefully, abysmally, monstrously, amazingly, stupefyingly, ineffably ... crap.'

'So you don't think you're very good at it, like.'

'I wouldn't put it as bluntly as that, but no.'

'Why?'

Now Weed wanted to marry Warren, ratting dogs and all. There had not been a trace of derision, scorn, anger or contempt in his question, just a simple wanting to know. Weed had spent so much time with Ms. Wap and the other trainers and supervisors of Daikon AirCon that he had become unaccustomed to conversation that did not include some veiled or overt attack on his competence as an employee and a human being.

'It's me. I'm not it. I don't have a salesman's personality. I don't even have a customer's personality. Blobby shaped peg in a square hole. That's me. I got a degree in physics. That's what did for me, that's why they stuck me in sales.

'With Daikon AirCon's placement criteria, Einstein would have been cleaning the toilets and a chimp with an honorary degree in poop tossing would be in charge of marketing strategies or payroll systems — and probably is.'

There was a slow thudding at the front door.

'You expecting Igor?' asked Warren. 'Or is the cat on barbiturates?'

Weed strode to the door, which took about one stride, and peered through the spy hole.

'See any spies in that hole?' Warren asked.

'Hello!'

'You should open the front door before you say hello. They can't hear you.'

'It's a prat.'

'Give the bloke a chance. How do you know he's a prat when you won't open the door to him? I think you're getting rude.'

'No, it's A. Pratt, that's his name, and he's totally wet. It's lashing down out there. I can't remember his first name. I work with him but he lives clear across town. I wonder what he wants.'

'Well don't keep us all in suspended animation. Open the door!'

Weed opened the door, which meant pushing Warren into the corner of the living room to make room for it.

'Hi, there. What brings you here?' Weed said brightly.

'I have to speak to you on a matter of some importance. I'm A. Pratt and I'm here to help you.'

Weed immediately recognised the Daikon pitch 'You are not seriously going to try to sell me an air conditioner, are you?'

'In the long dog days of summer when —' Pratt droned on through the pitch.

'Look, I'll save you from wasting your time here. Take a hint and get onto the next flat.'

' — actually protects the furniture from mould and skin rashes —'

'Better still, skip the entire block. You're more likely to catch TB than sell an air conditioner here.'

'— ensures a consistently high negative ion balance —'

'Look, I just don't want one.'

'— have been linked to lower rates of divorce and rapid career advancement —'

'Nobody needs one of those machines in this country. The whole market for them was created out of slick PR and gullibility.'

'— tomatoes grow faster and bigger —'

'They are a waste of resources and cause pollution.'

'— strengthening the bonds between you and other human beings —'

'They mess with the body's ability to cool itself and interfere with your immune system.'

'— only two hundred and fifty easy instalments and at no extra —'

'Look, there isn't a power in this universe that could make me buy one of those things.'

Pratt stopped at the end of his spiel and glared at Weed. He was obviously exhausted and had probably been on the job for fourteen hours. Water dribbled out of his hairline and dripped off his nose. He sniffed and shivered, his eyeballs rolled in folds of purple, bloated flesh. Legionnaire's disease. If you're slow with the boosters, it'll get to you every time.

'So you're not going to buy one, then, Weed.'

'No. I'm sorry.'

'You're screwed, Weed. Totally screwed.' And he went away.

'What's this?' asked Warren, still in the corner like a well-padded pediment. 'Has Joyful Encounters run out of ratting dogs and started sending out the rats instead?'

'Poor bloke. That's what I hate about this job, the abject futility of talking to people like me all day.'

Weed closed the door, freeing enough space for Warren to start circulating blood again.

'Right,' said Warren, 'how about a proper drink?'

'I shouldn't, but I know I'm going to anyway. Where're my hat and coat?

'You're standing on them.'

'Ah, yes. My amazing multi-functional overcoat. I use it as a carpet to save money. And the hat makes a nice little stool.'

There was a rapid thudding at the front door.

'You want to get that seen to, mate. It could turn nasty.'

Warren was pushed back into his corner and Weed hauled the door open.

Warren shouted helpfully through the crack, 'If that's a dead cat you got there, you can't swing it in here.'

'Good gracious, Mr. Scourge —' It was Mr. Scourge, Weed's field supervisor, with the rain battering around him. A fork of lightning savaged the night behind him and thunder startled the dishes in their drying rack.

'Good evening, sir. I understand you don't have an air conditioner.' Pratt was at his elbow wearing a smirk the size of the San Andreas fault.

'I —' said Weed

'Perhaps you'd like one. This is the model you would like.' He shoved a shiny brochure into Weed's hand.

'I —'

'Now, the good news is, since you are an actual employee of Daikon AirCon, we don't need to bother with financial plans. We'll just take it out of your salary.'

'I —'

'Just sign here.' Scourge offered his clipboard.

'I —'

'Thank you very much for your purchase. As an employee of Daikon AirCon, your loyalty to your company has been recorded and will be taken into account when your contract comes up for review and renewal.'

Weed signed.

'We'll be round to install it eventually.'

And he was off with Prat skittering behind him.

'That's the way to do it, you prat,' said Scourge.

'I see, sir. By the way, it's A. Prat, not U. Prat.'

'Let's be off, then.' said Warren. 'I'm paying, I think.'

'Scourge is not of this universe,' said Weed miserably.

The air conditioner that Weed bought is an iCon and has a network port so it can connect directly to the internet.

The air conditioner hangs on the wall. The estate agent had said it was a wall and was most keen to point it out. The air conditioner hangs on the wall and whispers to itself. When it doesn't whisper to itself it hums to itself. Occasionally for the hell of it, it will gurgle, mumble, creak, groan, or squeak to itself or make exasperated tut-tut-tutting noises. Weed was wondering whether the air conditioner was schizophrenic or just plain daft. Weed was also wondering how to turn the damn thing off. Once it was on, there seemed to be no stopping it. In this respect, it was exactly like the tv. Weed's dad had turned it on when it had been delivered and Weed had yet to find an off switch. He had to suppress it by draping his mattress over it, which made sleeping a chore.

Sometimes when the tv was cackling to itself like a busybody goose, and the air conditioner was whispering to it or huffing and gurgling and puffing, Weed would think the two of them were in cahoots, that they were encouraging each other, or especially that the air conditioner was encouraging the tv.

Why not the other way around? Why wasn't the tv encouraging the air conditioner? Well, I'm sure you have by now understood that this is a paranoid and unstable delusion and is therefore necessarily irrational, so why shouldn't the air conditioner be encouraging the tv?

But encouraging the tv in what?

Weed doesn't watch tv. He doesn't like it and mostly he doesn't have the time. Daikon AirCon has his time and they are not giving it back. Daikon AirCon is sucking him up and rearranging him in straight lines to their liking, night and day — rather like something going through an air conditioner.

Weed senior, Weed's dad, had insisted he have a tv. Buying the tv had been a thoroughly horrible experience all of its own.

'It is the heart and the hearth, the unifying, er ... thing, the unifying bit in the middle. The unifying principle. A home without a telly is like a castle without a keep, a trifle without sherry, a toilet without a seat, shoulders without a head. And what's the point of all that, eh?'

They were in the electrical things shop and Weed's dad was declaiming — loudly.

Weed had exhibited the temerity right there, surrounded by all those wonderful things, to suggest he might not want or need a tv. He had told his father quite frankly but not at all rudely that he didn't much like the box and that he didn't have the time to watch it, and when he did have the time he preferred to do other things such as build a tachyon drive in his bathroom.

Now Weed's father was gently remonstrating with him.

'How can you say that? Here we are in this treasury of home entertainment, this trove of electrical convenience, this ... this ... emporium of ... of ... discounted stuff, and you say you don't want a tv, that you've got better things to do with your time?

'Did you know that if the history of this planet was represented as one year, then the telly was invented on December 31st at 11.59 and 59 seconds, just when everybody was popping the bubbly. It therefore represents the pinnacle of a whole year's evolutionary struggle and carnivorism. And do you know why it took a whole year to invent? Because there was no tv to give us ideas. We had to think for ourselves. Think about it!

'It is estimated that in history a number of billions of people lived and died without setting eyes on or even hearing the name of tv. That's a number of billions of people, Robert. That's more people than you or I could shake a remote control at, lad. All these people who lived and died in mud huts and palaces alike, having to make their own entertainment with logs or bones or string quartets, and you in this wonderful pharmacopoeia have the bloody cheek and the selfish nerve to say that you don't want one 'cos you don't want one. Well, son, I say unto you, go send your peanuts back to Ethiopia.'

To help make his point, Weed's father climbed a twin-tub UltraKwik MegaKwiet washing machine and declaimed to the whole store.

'How can it be bad? I asks you, how can it be bad? Tv, after all begins with a crucifix. Not that we believe in all that bollocks, but it's the association. It denotes goodness and ... and nice things. And to them that says there's too much violence on tv, I say stick it up your arse!

'It represents peace because it's nice to watch it when you're relaxing after work and everyone shuts up their yacking when the telly's on.

'It represents love because we love to watch it.

'It represents harmony because everybody watches it together.

'It represents wisdom because the people who make the programmes are very clever to know all that stuff; and the telly is the information that saturates us.

'It represents truth cos the camera never lies.

'It teaches us self-discipline because we have to get up early to watch breakfast tv.

'It teaches us forgiveness, 'cos when the football is snowed off or when the cameramen go on strike they show those nice old movies with proper women in them like Audrey Hepburn and proper straight men like Cary Grant.

'How can it be a bad thing? Let us pray.

Our Father who art Television,
Hallowed be thy Schedule.
Thy kingdom is here.
Thy will is done,

On earth as it is on the Goggle.
Give us this day our daily fix.
And forgive us our lapses of attention
while we make the Brew,
As we forgive those who misplace the remote control.
And lead us into Temptation in the Ads and the Soaps,
But deliver us from thinking.
For Telly is the Kingdom, and the Power Switch and
the Glamour, for ever and ever,
Innit.

The customers and staff who had gathered round to hear Weed's dad burst into enthusiastic applause and glared at Weed.

Weed bought a tv.

Another thing the air conditioner has in common with the tv is that Weed doesn't use it much and if he can get them turned off, he tries to keep them off. He lives in a cold country and indeed the conditioner has a heating function, which might have been handy if the thing didn't actually make him ill. The heating function only warms the ceiling and gives him nausea and headaches because the clever engineers that designed it apparently didn't understand that hot air rises. Mr. Scourge his supervisor forced him to buy the conditioner. It was, along with the tv, a symbol of unity, a facilitator of loyalty, to the larger community.

Apart from the unnecessary expense and the debt, one of the reasons Weed didn't want to bother much with a telly or the other things that fascinated his parents was that he had plans for the free time he had very little of. Big plans. Huge plans. Plans that would barely fit on the planet.

Although the telly and the gadgets were unhelpful, one of his father's impetuous decisions had an unexpected advantage, had in fact enabled Weed's wild plans, and that was his father's insistence he buy the flat. In his parents' home he had only the space behind the sofa to call his own. There was not much chance of him doing anything there but picking fluff out of his hair and shooing away spiders. The new flat was not very big but it did have the advantage that he could open a book without barking his knuckles on the commode.

Weed planned, against his parents wishes, to be himself. Who knew, maybe he could even escape from Daikon AirCon and the Heavenly Estate. A substantial part of the senior Weed's HP plan was controversially rerouted by the junior Weed into books — specifically, a distance learning course in astronautics. Weed was going into space — assuming he passed the test. To go into space he needed to pass at least one test and there seemed to be rather a lot of training involved. But the training wasn't a problem for Weed, he was good at being trained; his training at Daikon AirCon had included a module called *Training for the Uninitiated: optimising the skills acquisition process* — Weed, in other words, had been trained to be trained — a skill he hadn't imagined would be transferable or even useful.

To pass the test he apparently needed books and had therefore used his salary to buy some even though they hadn't got through a quarter of the shopping list of essential consumer durables — of consumer unendurables, from Weed's point of view — his parents had helpfully drawn up for him. He had books on computers, books on astrophysics, books on spaceship engineering, books full of pictures of stars and planets so he would know one if he got into space and saw one; books on relativity, on particle and quantum physics; books on frogs, tomato growing and floating.

Inspired by his reading he had gone a massive step further. He figured he could make a spaceship engine and quickly made a good start on a working prototype tachyon drive in his bathroom.

A tachyon drive is a revolutionary spaceship engine that would propel a craft faster than the speed of light and therefore backward in time. This engine would also bring in huge amounts of money there being nothing else like it on the planet. However, money was not Weed's first interest in the project.

In the nature of the thing, the engine had appeared before he started work on it. It had simply been there one morning, travelling backward in time from some future test, blocking his view of the shaving mirror and leaving deep indentations in the soap. That was the morning after he had made his first concrete plans to make it and he was rather pleased to see it because it suggested he was on the right track.

The tachyon drive, when completed would solve our basic problems with space travel. The basic problem with space travel — apart from the high degree of impossibility attached to it — was the awful distances involved. Another huge problem was speed — not that astronauts were amphetamine fiends or anything. Travelling huge distances at the speed of light you sort of get ahead of yourself. Arriving back on earth, you find that your grandchildren are older than you and have much better salaries and more satisfying jobs. Seems that Time's winged chariot has its limits and perhaps hasn't kept up with progress. Weed's tachyon drive would get around this problem and many more. Tachyon's are apparently the only things in the universe that can go faster than the speed of light, and breaking light's speed rule, they are entitled to break another in that they are allowed to — indeed have to — go backwards in time. It follows that an engine that generates tachyons will also go backwards in time, thus solving the relativity problem by cancelling out the time distortion effect. We could zoom around the universe as much as we liked and still get back to beat our grandkids to those proper jobs.

The thing took over the bathroom, coming and going but reliably growing, with the result that he was always showering before he got dirty and always had to take the plug out of the bath for it to fill up with tepid water and then wait an hour for it to get hot before he could climb in.

Our young engineering nerd was immensely proud of his invention and like all the best machines, it was not so complicated. Here is a list of essential ingredients.

- *an old alarm clock*
- *a sprocket of regret*
- *a spring of hope*
- *some cogs of endeavour*
- *molecules*
- *atoms*
- *bicycle oil*
- *a 20x20 hindsight lens*
- *a keen sense of fun*
- *a cold fission power pack of unlimited output, hooked up to a portable and absolutely efficient particle accelerator*

The Weed family was very loyal; and their loyalty was recognised. They were rewarded: they were invited to the palace to be presented to the royalty and the priests. They were received into the inner chamber and inducted. They were baptised in a twenty-four hour, seven-day-a-week procession of baptisms. It was an affirmation of their own fealty and was conducted on behalf of all the others who couldn't be here with us tonight. Yes, the Weed family — Mr. and Mrs. Weed, and the junior Weed too — got themselves on telly. Yay!

Being on tv is, of course, about a lot more than going in front of a camera. The tv is to your humanity what the air conditioner is to air. The Weeds were sucked, hoovered clean by the camera; they were purified. As their stale and humid molecules shot into the machine and were rearranged in straight lines, they were buffed and polished and imbued with the magic only the tv medium can impart. Now they sparkle and gleam with fairy-dust ions. Weed and his parents are blessed; they are elect; they are lucky bastards — or as close as one can get without actually being a lucky bastard. Eventually, with their molecules all cleaned and shiny, they were beamed back at themselves, fired gently from the cathode tube at their sofa, where they were reassembled point by gleaming, sparkling point, until they were completely reconstructed, refreshed, renewed, reinvented; until they were reformed as grinning pillars of magic salt.

Since then, whenever they sit down with a piping brew and a pack of jammy tarts to watch the box, it is an act of communion because they are forever of it.

A week or so after the show was aired, Weed's parents came round to Weed's flat to see it on video. They hadn't yet seen their own appearance on tv because they were actually in it and the show had gone out live. It was mind-boggling irony that they had not seen their own show because they were in it, and an irony that they needed to repeat to people as often as possible, whether other people had any interest in having their minds boggled with irony or not.

Weed, however was grappling with an assignment. He was always grappling with assignments. It didn't matter that he was now an initiate; the training and the assignments went on regardless.

A day or two before the show was made word leaked out and for one whole awe-struck morning his tv adventure took some of the pressure off him at work. The tv magic was indeed potent. The story of Weed's audience with Sam Smiles had slipped out through his best friend and was networked all over the company before Weed could say 'Shut up, Warren!' The hectoring eased up: you don't give the blessed a hard time. But by lunchtime his new status was causing him new headaches: as one who has been touched it was expected that he become an example for all the trainees. After all, you were chosen for a reason; not just any bonehead got on tv. This man must have a hidden side, an aura only the tv people could detect, a vibration, a sign that marked him out as one of their own. So more was expected of him, yet he still had nothing to give. Even tv's magic was not powerful enough to make him a good salesman.

The evening the show was aired he had to write three to five thousand words titled *Strategy Augmentation Core 7, Client-Facing Establishment and Collocation: Deportment in Detrusion* — or how to sit nicely when talking to customers. The deadline was just one short night away, and his folks were coming round to watch themselves. He wouldn't have bothered having the telly on at all but his parents had insisted on making it a nice family occasion. In truth he had no desire to remember the nightmare of his baptism.

As the tv minutes ticked away and his parents held his attention by the scruff of the neck to the screen, he could see his essay growing into the night. He could see tomorrow's early start looming out of the morning fog as flexible and moveable as the Eurasian plate, and as friendly as a windscreen to a gnat.

Weed was dangling — being dangled — barely a metre above a vat of pink blancmange. The blancmange quivered expectantly. In Weed's day it was plain old custard in the dangling vat, and when he had pointed that out to the floor manager before the show he had been told that custard was "unbearably passé!" So quivering pink blancmange it was.

'What's the capital of Latvia?'

'Riga.'

'Correct! Well done!'

This was easy. Lots of questions before this had been easy.

'How do you spell "haemorrhage"?'

Weed spelled it. Most contestants were lobbed into the pink by this point, but Weed was still dangling on, rotating slowly but not getting queasy. To be honest, the pink of the blancmange was more upsetting to the stomach than the precarious dangling and rotating or the questions he was getting. The blancmange with its plastic, ectoplasmic quality could have been something secreted by Ms. Wap.

'Be careful now, Bob. This one might be tricky. What is Planck's wall?'

A doddle: that's what Planck's wall is.

'Ten to the power of minus twenty four of a second,' Weed told him.

'Can you elaborate?' Asked Sam Smiles warily. The audience gasped unanimously and loudly: get elaborate? You mean get fancier than quoting that number off the top of your head?

'It is a theoretical point in time after the Big Bang, before which the laws of physics as we know them don't seem to apply.'

'Absolutely correct!' boomed Mr. Smiles.

'Last question, Bob. If you get this one right all of these lovely prizes are for you. And your family. To take home with you.'

Get on with it, Smiles, Weed thought. There'll be no time for the last question if you keep drivelling on.

'Sabrina, just one more quick look at those prizes to remind us what is quite literally hanging in the balance.'

The prizes could be found behind a huge three-dimensional plastic rendering of the very smiling head of Sam Smiles. The big plastic head would revolve to reveal what everyone wanted, so the trove of goodies appeared to be located where Smiles' brain ought to be found. Slightly bizarre if one thought about it too closely, but great subliminal PR if one didn't.

And here are the prizes now: the great big head spins gracefully on its axis and so does its plastic simulacrum. And what a lot of shiny things the Weeds have amassed here tonight, mainly thanks to Weed's braininess and Weed senior's skill at swallowing living gerbils and regurgitating them unharmed.

The audience was duty bound to ooh and aah whenever glimpsing the prizes in the show. Oohs were one of the conditions of use listed on the back of the free tickets, and aahs were another condition listed there. Technically, failure to comply would render your ticket invalid. In practice, the good folks of the audience needed no instruction or encouragement.

The audience oohs and aahs and ululates. A couple of people rush the stage and have to be held back by the security but they only want to touch the prizes or Sam or Mr. Weed or even a mike stand. Such a horde of nice things has not been collected on even this show before. Here we see an Everest, a whole Himalayas of gifts, all ready to be packed up in the waiting U-haul that is bigger than the Weed's flat — we have seen the lorry already waiting behind the studio with its yellow hazard lights spinning and flashing and its phalanx of Group Security 4 Us outriders and tv vans revving.

There must be two or three rotisseries here and a trip for forty-seven to Irkutsk. There's a cuddly anaconda and a large labour-free plastic cheese plant. You will find coupons for free dental care once you turn eighty or lose all your teeth whichever happens first, and a tachometer specially designed for shoes which will tell you when you need your footwear replacing, where you were the night before and will keep you apprised of your cholesterol levels

'And of course you already have the cow and you'll be taking that home with you whatever the outcome. Of the next question.

'One more look at that beautiful cow please Sabrina.'

A plastic shell like a big pink vulva opens to show us the cow, festooned in Hawaiian garlands and dotted with stick-on sequins. The cow looked doleful and wondered whether there was enough of itself to feed all those people there.

'So here it is. The last question: a famous 1986 film starring Tom Cruise as a US Navy fighter pilot is called *Top* ... what?

Weed was thrown so completely off guard that he nearly toppled into the blancmange without any help from Smiles' pearl-handled dunking lever. The audience bayed and howled and began shouting something like "Gun! Gun!"' at him. He had no idea why they were shouting "gun" at him and concluded he must be hearing "go on" but somewhat mangled by the acoustics in the studio. He wondered briefly at the folly of allowing such treacherous acoustics in a hall designed specifically for recording in and then shut out the pandemonium to apply himself to the question.

'You must answer, Bob. The seconds are ticking away!'

Tom who? thought Weed. Pynchon? Mann? Hardy? Wolfe? Aquinas? A Beckett? A Kempis? Cat? Brehm? Jones? Ato? Surely none of them made a film.

Mentally he scanned his parent's extensive video collection for help. There it is, up there on the top shelf in the living room, in pride of place. *Singing in the Rain*, *The Sound of Music* and *West Side Story*.

'We've got the lot now,' Mr. Weed had said when he had won the boxed set of three in the raffle at the pub. Mr. Weed was into winning things and was very good at it except when it really mattered.

'How's that, love?' asked Mrs. Weed.

'Look, it says so here on the box. "Regal ParlourView: The definitive and comprehensive video collection." Look no further love. We've got the lot right here in our hands. Well I have.' And he sighed proudly.

'We'll have to be getting a video machine to be playing them on, then, won't we.' She didn't have to ask how much that would cost. They spent most Saturdays in the electrical things shop keeping vigil before the video machines with a pocket calculator borrowed from the nearby display calculating and recalculating HP scenarios. They never did manage to make the numbers work without doing away with something like food or heat. But it looks like they're going to get lucky tonight. There are at least four VCRs in the prize pile, and there was a fair to middling chance that one of them was designed for use in this country.

And their clever son was answering all the questions. Except he was being a bit slow with this last one.

The fact was, Weed didn't know the answer to the question that would allow them to take home all the wonderful prizes. But there was no problem. Weed was deciding to reason this one out. He was good at that sort of thing.

'Robert?'

Lets try logical association: spot the concept that fits. OK. US navy. Fighter pilot. Top boat — top fighter — top pilot — top mach three —top war — top planes — top bombs — top death — top mutilation — top blood — top people screaming — top body parts strewn across streets and fields — top babies in rubble — top profits ...

'You must answer now, Robert. The film was called *Top* ...?'

'Hat?' ventured Weed and splat he went, right into the blancmange where he floundered and glubbed while the audience howled with delighted horror.

Weed's mother clenched her fists, clenched her shoulders, clenched her elbows, clenched her face and screamed. His father set his mouth in a grim line, tried looking liberal-but-firm but gave up and defaulted to one of his what-do-they-teach-kids-in-schools-these-days expressions.

Sam Smiles put his arms around Mrs. Weed as if comforting a bereaved person and beamed cheerily.

'Well that's life on Get a Life! The Weed family have come such a long way tonite to be here and came such a long way in the game of life we played here tonite as we do at the same time every Saturday nite only to fall at the last hurdle — or in Robert's case, fall into the last hurdle — Robert come round here and join us — we come into this life with nothing and these lovely people certainly aren't taking any of it. Away with them. Tonite!

'Sabrina — one more look at all the beautiful things they didn't win here tonite. Isn't that a crying shame?'

And was Mr. Weed crying just a wee bit there behind his stoic and dignified exterior? Certainly, he was sufficiently distracted to not notice when the cry of alarm went up. The floor staff and the bunny girls had just noticed that the dunked Weed had not re-emerged from the pink glop. A klaxon lifted its skirts and screamed like a startled elephant. A brigade of uniformed guards bearing fire extinguishers bore down on and surrounded the vat of blancmange and were immediately backed up by several emergency camera crews.

The blancmange, normally fat and jolly and pink and not at all unlike Inspector Yard, now with a man trapped inside, seemed malevolently postprandial and sated, and still not at all unlike Inspector Yard.

This is how Sam got to first hear of the problem. A voice in his wireless, electronic ear said, 'Balls-up stage centre. The sap's gonna croak. Or glug as the case might be.'

This is how Sam reported the news. 'Hold on a moment, good people — we have a real live situation on the stage. On the show. Here tonite. As I speak. It seems that our plucky contestant has not yet re-emerged from the from the Batty Vat. He entered here and was supposed to exit here or in this general vicinity but he is still down there. In there. Out of sight. We have no idea what condition he may be in not hungry one would guess and certainly not short of wholesome sugar because here on Get a Life and unlike other shows on other channels we use only the real article yes fine top quality edible blancmange with nothing artificial taken away of course as ever provided by the good people of FishEye Dream Toppings and Fertilisers so you can nip to any good retail outlet and pick up some of the self-same blancmange to enjoy anytime in the privacy and comfort of your own home but not right now because you'll be wondering what has happened to Robert. Our contestant. Here tonite.

'I can assure you good people that this is completely. Unplanned entirely. Unscheduled.

'And you can see here Robert's poor family — distraught with worry wondering whether they will ever see their beloved first and only born again alive because we are sure to find him eventually because we are all professionals here and no mistake.

'This is right isn't it, love, he's your only child and you're so worried you're going to need trained paramedics to give you oxygen and a blanket.

'And you, Mr. Weed, how exactly do you feel? First missing out on all those lovely things and then seeing your first and only die horribly ... and we may assure you there will be hard questions asked tonite in the offices of tv stations all over the world about whether the change from custard to blancmange was really justifiable and whether the human 'cost is, er ... justifiable or whether it was just another cost raising ploy to justify higher ad rates but here on Get a Life we maintain only the strictest safety protocols everything is thought of nothing left to chance except the jokes which have not been tested on a representative sample of a mere three million of the nation's population beforehand by the worthwhile. And erstwhile. Poll specialists Gallivant and NOPE.

'Your safety while watching this fast and sometimes furious game of life — and today death — just like real life itself — is paramount as is the safety of our guests our contestants and the hardworking staff and crew on this show who selflessly slave away. Behind the scenes. Without a shred of credit.'

Several of the crew that labours without credit were now clearing a path through a larger crowd of the crew that labours without credit and the bunny girls. They were making way for a gaggle of clean and earnest young men clad in big rubber suits and carrying oxygen tanks and flippers.

'And now give a big hand ladies and gentlemen for these men of the Royal Marine Commandoes and before these fine men the nation's finest swing into action and show us how it's done. Let me just introduce. One or two. Of them.

'Excuse me, sir, might I briefly divert you from your mission of mercy? Would you like to tell the folks at home your name?

'Certainly. I'm Marine Lieutenant Michael Goodboy.

'I don't believe that's the way your team addresses you. What do they call you?'

'Sir.'

'Yes,' prompted Sam. 'And when they're not calling you sir they're calling you ...'

'Madam?'

'Or ... ?'

'Or?'

'I believe I'm referring to your nickname.'

'Oh, I see.'

Silence.

'Which is?'

'Er, that would be 'Mad' Mike.'

'And why would they call you that?'

'Because it's my nickname, Sam.'

'Yes, but why that particular nickname?'

'I've no idea, Sam. Perhaps it's because it's alliterative with my given name.'

'Great, Lieutenant Goodboy. And could you briefly introduce the rest of your team?'

'Oh, certainly. This is Sergeant Julian Chap ...'

'By nickname? I believe you all have rather interesting nicknames.'

'Oh right. This is, erm, 'Mad' Julian, 'Mad' Sebastian, and 'Mad' Crispin.'

'Thank you so much, Lieutenant 'Mad' Mike Goodboy. And now what are you going to do?'

'We're going to rescue the boy.'

'And how exactly are you going to do that?'

'We plan to leap into action without a moment's hesitation, leap swiftly and professionally into the custard — '

'Blancmange.'

' — blancmange — and executing a series of carefully planned and well-rehearsed manoeuvres, we will locate the boy and transfer him to safety.'

'And there's not a second to lose, am I right?'

'That's right, Sam.'

'So this is pretty dramatic.'

'No, all of it is entirely real. We are professionals.'

'But this kind of operation must be a doddle for you, right?'

'A what?'

'A doddle —'

'You mean like an egg boiled in a cup? Yes, it might be a bit like that.'

'A doddle, Mike — something easy.'

'Well, as I say, Sam, you are the professional, and, er ...'

'Right, let's see you going through those professional paces because we have a commercial break coming up in just a few minutes.'

A searchlight was trained on the surface of the gloop and the ring of guards was broken to allow the heroes access to the pudding. The Commandoes, clutching their face masks sat on the edge of the Batty Vat and toppled backwards into the big pink.

The dessert's surface roiled and oxygen tanks and flippers sleeked across its surface. The Commandoes were doing an admirable imitation of cavorting dolphins or perhaps black olives being energetically laundered with a lot of pink satin shirts.

Abruptly, Weed's floppy and inert body was expelled and dragged roughly out and splatted on the stage. Paramedics sat on his back and pumped and pounded his thorax.

Weed was unconscious but his face had reflexively defaulted to a number one smile, the smile for people who were sure they wanted an air conditioner. A camera edged in close under a medic's elbow to catch as much as possible of this real life death until its lens was pinked out by a thick blob of blancmange ejected with great force from Weed's trachea by the pounding medics.

Stage right, forgotten bewildered and alone we find the cow, the only thing the Weeds will be taking home with them. It has on a glitzy, sequined tutu and a fez, it has Hawaiian garlands around its neck and there is a pile of dump on the dais behind it.

Already the station's switchboard was jammed with calls complaining about the unscheduled presence of horror on prime time and offers of work for 'Mad' Mike Goodboy to appear in tv commercials for chocolate and coffee. The people calling about the horror on the show were not complaining about the live near death, they were complaining about Weed's obscene number one snarl.

Ushered from the tv studio at show's end the Weed family were at last placed in a taxi at the show's expense. There were some tense minutes outside the studio when Smiles had insisted that the staff find the Weeds a taxi with a horsebox. Eventually Mrs Weed had piped up that this was dead silly and of course they were getting nowhere, because what they really need was a taxi with a cow box. When that didn't work, they went for any old taxi, which the staff found easy to deal with because Smiles was bored and had gone back inside the studio. This was Mr. Weed's first trip in a taxi and he would have been terribly excited if it had been under any other circumstances. As it was, it didn't even start out as compensation. And he knew full well that the station was paying only because his son's near drowning had put the ratings for the night through the roof.

They lashed the cow to a handle of the taxi and drove very slowly back home with the beast being compelled to follow.

On the way, Weed's parents decided that the animal should stay with their son because there was no grass around their estate and anyway Weed was the soft one.

So back at the heavenly estate, Weed chained up the cow in the bike sheds. There was plenty of free space because all the bikes had long since been stolen. The next morning the cow was still there. It was covered with graffiti but otherwise OK.

Weed decided to call the cow Ermintrude. It was Ms. Wap's first name.

That was our hero's first and only appearance on tv, and that's how the Weeds came by the family cow.

As Weed cringed and sweated in front of the box his essay went undone. On the other hand, his parents watching themselves seemed to have forgotten the comprehensiveness of that night's catastrophe. They may not have won the prizes, but they had been on television; and now they had seen themselves on television. They had seen themselves up there on the stage with Sam Smiles and all sorts of beautiful people; they had seen themselves woven into the sparkling tapestry as if it was their natural environment. They were more than content.

Eventually when the senior Weeds had finished rerunning, analysing and dissecting the show, they put on their coats and went in search of a night bus.

Weed now got stuck into his essay. As arduous and infuriating as the task might be, at least it drove away the trembling memory of the Sam Smiles show, and hunched over his little kitchen table, he could at least fantasise that he was an artist in his garret, or a terribly ascetic academic working on something thought-provoking and worthwhile.

Alas the reality was, as it reliably is, something other. Weed's essays are basically what Ms. Wap tells him in training — or as much of it as Weed can remember — with a few moderate embellishments of his own.

Let's take a peek over Weed's shoulder and see how Daikon AirCon uses his intellect and his evenings.

Strategy Augmentation Core 7, Client-Facing Establishment and Collocation: Deportment in Detrusion

One should not consider sitting to be a mere matter of convenience or a labour-saving strategy. The humble act of sitting is potentially one of the more powerful elements in our armoury of sales weapons. As with all activities and aspects of the environment apparently incidental to the larger sales task, careful attention must be paid to the ways in which we are able to extract and exploit maximum strategic and tactical potential.

Our deportment and presentation are as much part of the overall branding of our machines as the accoutrements of top-end or primary marketing. The way we sit is, as much as the clothes we wear, a statement about who we are, why we are there, and what enhancement we can bring to the customer's life through our service.

In a sense, to sit is to stand: it is our strong and assertive and proud customer-visible front [finish this bit later]

One should sit with both one's buttocks on the seat. When in the home of a potential customer whose social mores and preferences are different from one's own, one should sit with both buttocks on the floor.

Accurate and efficient placement of the buttocks can be facilitated by the simple expedient of a swift, discreet reconnoitring glance at the designated sitting surface to establish its dimensions, height and location relative to proximate objects — especially those objects that may be a potential source of embarrassment in collision scenarios, such as table lamps, domestic pets, objet d'art or fruit knives.

It is generally unnecessary to deploy measuring or surveying equipment such as tape measures, spirit levels or theodolites during the reconnaissance stage of sitting. While doing so would convey a strong image of professionalism and diligence, the client is usually in a state of anticipation to hear about your products and may prefer not to wait.

From the erect, detrusion can be accomplished thus. Shift one's centre of gravity forward by inclining the torso no more then fifteen degrees. This is to obviate a rearward topple when the thigh muscles contract to lower the posterior onto the designated sitting surface. It is necessary to permit a concomitant contraction of the calf muscles, which will facilitate an angling of the knees. If this part of the procedure is overlooked the result may be a bow rather than a sit.

Having safely established oneself in a sitting mode, posture becomes important. The way you sit can convey a huge amount of information and can positively or adversely influence the vendition.

As Weed wrote he began to feel poisoned. It was a feeling he frequently experienced at work: dried out and toxic, mouth rimed with slime, headache, regiments of ants or tiny, hyperactive worms crawling around in the capillaries of his chest, through the skin of his face, filling his throat. At first he attributed it to being microwaved by the fluorescent lights and the computer monitors and the mobile phones. He attributed it to the serried regiments of air molecules and germs and vestigial manufacturing chemicals that were ushered from the air conditioners and the lack of opportunity for proper, natural physical movement in his job. He worried it might be Legionnaire's — a continual hazard for any one so intimately involved with air conditioners or anyone just on the same planet as one. Along with all the new recruits he had been vaccinated when he joined the company but he went for his booster shots early. They made no difference. It may have been that the virus had mutated again but this would have hospitalised thousands by now. He attributed the feeling to Sick Building Syndrome. When he realized the feeling was following him outside into the field and following him home, he attributed it to Sick World Syndrome.

Generally, sitting upright is recommended, but the professional salesmanperson should take its cue from the client and be prepared to interpret and adapt to his or her preferences. Thus draping oneself over the back or across the arms or seat of a chair are not recommended unless explicitly requested by the client.

A straight back conveys strength, assertiveness and direction while a round back suggests indecisiveness, weakness and cancer. The symbolism of a hoop is of on-goingness or even infinity and may subliminally suggest to the client that he or she will be in this sales situation for an indefinite or eternal period of time thus causing anxiety that they might be late for that crucial VIP lunch or miss tonight's instalment of Coronation Street.

However, some commentators (Weed, 2008) have suggested that this symbolism may impact favourably on the client's longevical expectations of the product, especially after the recent unfair press Daikon AirCon has received about the reliability of some of the core products, and their alleged tendency to kill users and destroy the planet.

We might observe that the straight-backed posture is tried and tested while other spinal forms may introduce an element of radicalism or even the avante garde, the effect of which is somewhat unpredictable.

Men may want to cross their legs at the knees. This is perfectly acceptable. However, placing an ankle on a knee presents an overly confident and assertive aspect, leaving the client with the impression that he or she is not in control of the situation.

Moreover, resting one's ankle on one's knee may expose the sole of one's foot to the client. While Christians, Jews, most animists, Hindus, agnostics and atheists may be untroubled by this, a great many Muslims and Buddhists will feel offended.

Weed was proud of that bit. Most of his essay — any essay he wrote — parroted whatever Ms. Wap had told them in training, but this was information Weed had that Ms. Wap didn't. And in terms of Daikon AirCon's ongoing quest to appeal to everyone in the world, it was real scoop. He had made a point of asking Ms. Wap about this in the training.

'Might people get offended by your souls, Bob? Don't be silly. Souls are invisible — and we only have one each. Anyway, you shouldn't be discussing metallurgy with the client. Different points of view can be detrimental to the task in hand.'

Weed had tried not parroting Ms. Wap in his essays in his first weeks and months at Daikon AirCon. He would take the topic and run with it. He would run with it to the library, the internet and veteran sales staff, if he could catch them. He would run with it to his imagination, grabbing up his initiative as he went. And once the essay had been marked and returned to him he would find he had one point out of a possible hundred for spelling his name right and he would be derided for the rest of his effort. The content of his essay was all extra to what Ms. Wap had told them in training and was therefore either stuff she thought he didn't need to know or it was stuff the trainers didn't know and so irrelevant, suspect, or just plain fictitious in their eyes.

As a result of all the effort he expended on his essays, while most of the trainees were fatigued, Weed was exhausted and hallucinated pillows and cushions where other people saw tabletops, walls, shoulders and clients.

Eventually he realised that the essays and assignments were not there for him to develop his understanding of the subject. No, the assignment was there to make sure that the trainees had been listening to Ms. Wap all day and that they hadn't been dreaming of their sweethearts or a beach or a better job, that they hadn't slipped into catatonia or died.

Every evening they had to write down everything they had heard during the day, to demonstrate that they had not just absorbed all of it but had absorbed all of it in just the way Ms. Wap — or more accurately her own trainers — wanted.

The essays were more prescription: another technique for stilling all distracting thought or desire in Daikon's happy employees. The assignments are to education, growth and development what painting by numbers is to fine art. The process of submission to these futile tasks was the practice and demonstration of self-abnegation: leave your self in the umbrella stand on the way in.

Therefore even Weed's scoop about the soles of the feet might yet have to be excised before the essay is turned in. Knowing stuff is equivalent to attitude. Attitude is the one-word sentence to corporate oblivion. Attitude is equivalent to the Medieval pronouncement of 'unclean'; attitude is to the company what terrorism is to peace and stability. And Weed was attributed buckets of attitude by his trainers and elders and betters.

Weed made no more progress with the essay that night. He dozed off head down in the ashtray, where he dreamed of trying to sit bolt upright between the pink blancmange breasts of a huge Ms. Wap.

Does Weed dream? On the whole, in order to dream we need to sleep, though this is not an absolute rule. That this is not an absolute is an inconvenience we shall overlook here for reasons that may not become apparent.

Sleep is a time for regeneration and renewal, sleep sets the rhythm of the passing of our days; it fits in with breakfast, the slog, the dinner and the telly. Sleep takes time and presupposes the suspension of activity or the leisure to suspend activity. Sleep is for people who have a life.

Weed has no life and his daily rhythm is that of a startled bat in a locked wardrobe.

Sleep for Weed is brief moments of concussion, spots and patches of amnesia that punctuate his frantic batting about. Sleep is dark patches of dead time between better-lit patches of dead time.

Where for most people sleep is something to be relished, to be anticipated, to be pampered with cocoa, kisses or a good book, something to be taken in private between clean sheets and hopefully next to a cuddly body, for Weed, sleep is something involuntary and abrupt, something quite alarming that ambushes and mugs him, something that lurks as dark sucking pits distributed randomly through the city. He doesn't know when or where or whether sleep will appear beneath his feet and swallow him.

Nor does Weed ever know what sleep will do to him; sleep has the same zealous love of humiliation as Ms. Wap. Sleep may claim him on the train and may leave him slumped and sucking on the fly of the gent in the next seat. It may seize him in the supermarket and leave him sprawled between the shelves hugging a jumbo pack of toilet rolls. One attack of sleep took him in a customer's living room and in his unconsciousness Weed climbed the stairs, peed on the customer's bed and curled up obliviously in the customer's bathtub.

Ms. Wap and everyone else had something to say about that.

Yet Weed dreamed. To dream is to be human; to be human is to dream. We have no say in the matter. They say that to deprive yourself of sleep is to invite madness. Some people will insist until frothing at the mouth that the moon imparts insanity. Clearly this is nonsense. We dream at night because our heads fill up with insanity during the day while we are awake. Along with life-giving heat and light, the sun radiates tiny particles of insanity that enter through the eyes or ears or mouth and lodge in our minds. How many times have you finished work on the edge of idiocy or violence, how often have you sat on the train or in your car and felt the urge to blow big raspberries or make blubbery noises on your lips with a finger? Case proven.

It is evident then that when we sleep all the insanity drains away; it dribbles away unnoticed into the dark. If we fail to dream — fail to have dreams — the insanity gets thicker and thicker, until it fills up all the nooks and corners of our heads and no amount of sleeping is enough to make it go away.

Thus, having no alternative, Weed dreamed. Weed dreamed while his train was hurtling beyond his stop to the end of the line; he dreamed while he was hideously late for work. Sometimes he dreamed when he was apparently awake: as he spoke to clients, colleagues, or waiters, his unconscious would seep out. Weed would leak insanity right there, wherever he was, whoever he was talking to. It was embarrassing.

Waiters, the staff at fast food joints and other authority figures would appear to him as Waps or Stonewalls. Sales reps and shop clerks would become his parents. He started at the sight of them, told them he would have his assignment ready by eight tomorrow, told them he didn't need another bloody rotisserie; shouted at them, flailed his arms to beat them down and away, without use or effect. Old ladies selling newspapers on the street corners became those witches and Valkyries that chase you in your dreams through forests and gothic ruins until you realise your legs don't work at all and you lay gyrating like a wingless, legless fly in bed — or in Weed's case on the pavement outside the post office. Shadows became tall buildings that toppled on him as he passed. Buses became derelict ruins that swayed until they shook ghosts and sales manuals from the walls. On the other hand, teapots became cushions and downy four-poster beds, while the dregs of tea might appear as Bobette laughing and calling to him from the distance of a telescope.

But not all Weed's dreams were these waking hallucinations. Once in a while he gets his full eight minutes sleep. And what does he dream then? Well, he is dreaming now. Let's just creep in and have a peek.

I know this is a gross invasion of privacy but, to be honest, we haven't left much of himself to Weed; he belongs not to himself, he belongs to Daikon AirCon, he belongs to Ms. Wap and Slater Stonewall and his parents, he belongs to me, he belongs to you. We have picked him up and thrown him about and humiliated him at will, we have tortured him, deprived him of comfort or release — why not now barge into his innermost mind and plunder his dreams too?

We are now going to see that his dreams are full of the hackneyed images of an exhausted imagination, each dream a little dictionary of the clichés of the unconscious.

Weed is dreaming of stillness of peace, of simply being as opposed to being hassled or being tired or being persecuted or just being fed up.

Weed is lying on his back, he is outside and the sky rushes over him. The clouds are like airborne steamrollers. Weed is lying on his back and is not moving, not outside or in. He is staring at the sky fixed on some point that has meaning only for him, or his eyes may not be open at all. Weed is lying on his back as if crucified on the earth. Green things sprout around him, wriggling out of the ground. He is lying in a big field of grass and weeds and the weeds are excited to see him, they are welcoming him home. The weeds gather from the ground and wrap him up, cover him, smother him, tie him down and drag him into the earth.

Weed is at home, Weed is at peace, Weed is no more.

There is dark. The weed is extinguished, the weed is assimilated, the weed can begin to grow. Curled and knotted around himself — perhaps his thumb is in his mouth — he gets bigger and rounder and still there is peace and quiet and being; still there is still.

Now Weed stands or sits or squats as a big, fat turnip with a cute green mop of leaves on his head, and a tail-like, little umbilical thing dangling below.

He experiences a feeling beyond peace — the liberation that only peace brings; the elation that freedom and simply being brings.

And the peace is uplifting and fills the Weed-turnip like helium — and in a moment of insight and a simple effort of will — with a simple imagining, there he goes, off the ground and out of the tangle of weeds and vines, free of the corporeal slough, far from the madding clod, to bounce and bob on currents, to waft with spring's breath and dance with its eddies.

Eventually the floating turnip realises that with another little effort of will, another puff of elation, he can do more, and with a small sideways thought the leaves on his head begin to flutter and they begin to flap. Up, up he goes into the vault of blue.

Below, the green earth is like a blotchy, spoiled apple and he is leaving it behind.

The leaves on his head thrum and beat and now he can soar and swoop and zoom and loop the loop. Climbing high above the snaggle-toothed mountains, he patrols with the condor, descending into the broccoli hills, he flutters with the butterflies and plays tag with the sunbeams.

Practising his eagle eye, he spots far off another flying thing, big and round and moving with familiar helium bounces: it is another like him, all round and turnippy, and it has the same fun leaf-wings as he.

The Weed-turnip flies over to meet the new friend. There is no introduction. They are made for each other, so now the pair of them cavort together like big, happy balloons. They chase, tag, bump and slalom through the trees and vales. This is freedom. This is doing stuff. This is happiness, this is life.

From the spotless vault comes a single puffy white cloud that has come out to play with them, and the two flying turnips race over to say hello.

A single fluffy white cloud has detached itself from the stampeding herds of clouds above to come and play with them. It is a baby cloud that is bored with the stern march of the adult clouds and has come down to play with these two fun things that look and don't look like clouds. Now there are the three of them chasing each other all over the sky.

Around and around they go in a whirling play-dance that takes them in frantic, frenetic gyrations across the Toy Town countryside and closer and closer to the sun and into the summery breeze.

As they get closer to the sun, we come to see that it is not the burning ball of hydrogen millions of miles away as we had expected, but no more or less than the power light on a huge air conditioner set upon the horizon from which emanates the beautiful breeze. The air conditioner is a novelty model specially made for those with a keen sense of humour and this one in particular is made in the likeness of Ms. Wap's head. The power light is right in the middle of the forehead, and her mouth is open to expel the cool breezes they are all enjoying. But they are getting a little too close to the sun and the mouth now, and the nice breeze is turning into a bit of a gale. The wind picks them up and turns them around and suddenly their happy band is sundered, with Weed's turnip friend carried off one way and Weed and the cloud another.

With all the fun and the chasing around and now this sudden alarm at the air conditioner, the little cloud suddenly needs a tinkle, and a little tinkle it does right over the Weed-turnip. Not to worry. Baby cloud tinkle is but an April shower and not the yucky stuff at all. But then why does this stuff taste like disinfectant and why is it getting heavier and heavier?

Weed splutters awake to find he is on a train which has been shunted into a siding in the depot and is being hosed down inside and out by indifferent operatives in noddy suits on minimum wage.

By the time the Parks and Benches Operatives had finished their tea, the plant, the forest, the thing — the 'wotsit' they had dubbed it — had made even more progress. Its creepers were well past the operatives' feet. Testosteroni ground the green feelers under his boot heel and wished the council workers would get on with it.

Eventually they did take a break from the tea and further psyched themselves up by testing their scythes and secateurs on bits of the awful wotsit, quickly deciding after all that what was really needed was a good dose of paraquat. Reg said he had a can of the stuff back at the depot on a shelf behind some tins of as yet un-nicked corporation yellow paint that had been superseded by corporation orange, where he had placed it out of the way of the depot cat and the depot glue sniffers. The others agreed they remembered the shade of corporation yellow well, and lamented its passing to make way for the orange, which was a less sophisticated and an altogether brash colour by comparison. Then Reg fetched his bicycle and was off, escorted by a phalanx of police cars and motorcycle outriders with sirens screaming and lights flashing.

His colleagues decided on a cup of tea to mark the change of pace.

Before Reg returned, the wotsit had begun to occupy the neighbouring towers and the Heavenly Estate was beginning to look like a jungle mountain range.

It seemed to Weed that he had just got home when he found himself in his customary panic to get back out the door and back to work again. He paused with his toast in his mouth to adjust his tie in the mirror and to check that his appearance was, as usual, as scruffy as a hedge that had been dragged backwards through a larger and scruffier hedge.

Weed had a tie-adjusting mirror. The mirror didn't adjust Weed's tie knot, he did that himself while looking in the mirror. It would be a fine thing if the mirror adjusted your tie knot for you: imagine if you could make and market such a thing, imagine how much money you would make. If Weed could invent such a mirror and then find the capital to get it made and marketed, he might be able to give up being an air conditioner salesman. But he's not in mirrors — he will be soon but he doesn't know that yet. Not that he has a lot of free time. If a tie knot-adjusting mirror were a reality, lots of men wouldn't bother getting married. No, the mirror did not adjust the tie for Weed. That would be silly. Weed looked in the mirror when adjusting his tie.

Every morning on his way out of his flat Weed would stop and adjust his tie in this mirror — or rather, he would pause in headlong flight to wiggle his knot from left to right just to confirm it was today, like every other day, unable to hang dead centre where everyone else's tie hangs.

What Weed's knot lacked in centrality, it made up for in knottiness. Where his colleagues' knots were plump and primp and tended in shape to the conical or triangular, Weed's was a knotty kind of knot. It was the kind of knot caused by an impatient nine year old trying to undo the laces on his football boots, the kind of knot that could only be unravelled with an IQ of 180, a pair of shears, and a hammer and chisel. It was, in fact, the knottiest kind of knot.

Weed wasn't very good at tying ties despite staying up whole nights Windsoring and re-Windsoring. He just wasn't a tie-tying person, and it was his persistence and determination that installed the mirror by the front door. He thought with the mirror there to aid him he might be able to get his knots sorted out and be able to carry to work one small grain of confidence. Instead the sight of this intractable conundrum of polyester depressed him further and left him more acutely aware of his shambolic appearance. Only a rich and daft philanthropist with a thing for street people would buy an air conditioner from Weed. Our hero did not feel so much that his future was hanging in the balance, more that it was hanging from his neck at an unsightly angle.

Not that Weed was slovenly. Far from it. Weed was very diligent; it just seemed always that in Weed diligence brought about different results than in other people. When he groomed his hair it would develop whiplash and stand bolt upright. When he polished his shoes the soles would fall off. When he bathed he would get a rash from the soap. When his sales pitches were upbeat he came over fawning and ingratiating yet when he moderated his pitches he came over as moribund and diseased.

So on this particular morning, on this particular panicked flight to work he paused as was his custom to prod the rusty bedsprings of his hair and to unfurl his collar and to jiggle the impossible knot of his tie.

In the mirror he plumped the immaculate tie, adjusted a single hair that was microscopically out of place in his perfect rug, admired the pristine depilation of his chin, sneered at himself with supercilious contempt, and dived out the door.

As he slammed the door behind him it belatedly sank in that the image staring back at him from the mirror was a clean shaven un-pimpled, bright-eyed, kempt Weed with a perfectly triangular and conical tie knot.

He rummaged his keys from his floppy overcoat and stepped back in the house to double check his reflection to find his regular drooping self staring back at him from the mirror. He decided that his self-esteem was playing silly buggers with him.

Going back to check his mirror like that put him a whole thirty seconds behind schedule, he missed his usual train and was castigated by Ms. Wap. Yet the mystery apparition stayed in his memory all day — he was sure he had seen something odd and was not hallucinating. When he got home he sprang through the door as if expecting to catch the mirror conspiring with one-eyed bandits, dancing with fairies, or rummaging in his underwear drawer. However, the man who wasn't there wasn't there again, but how Weed wished he'd go away when he was there again the next day.

It was the same familiar but alien face: spruced, buffed, and glowing. Weed wasn't going to make the same mistake in lingering for a proper gawp and incurring the wrath of Wap, but once outside the flat he did indulge in a fleeting reflexive pause. He thrust a hand thoughtfully into a deep pocket of his overcoat and toyed with the fingers there.

He was leaping down the stairs to bypass the inevitably stalled lifts when it occurred to him to wonder why there were fingers in his coat pocket. Appalled, he halted and gingerly extracted the fingers, which were part of a hand — an actual hand, not a toy hand or a trick hand or a hand of cards or bananas. It was a hand that was actually alive and warm and moving. Unlike the living hands that Weed was familiar with that terminated at the wrist with a whole person, this one simply terminated at the wrist. Where the whole person should have been there was a glossy pink stub.

Evidently, the hand did not like being dangled gingerly and abruptly grasped Weed's wrist like an insecure baby monkey clinging to its mother.

Weed screamed and hopped about on the stairs trying to shake free the thing. The hand gripped him tighter so he tried running down the stairs rather than hopping about and he tried howling rather than screaming, but the hand held him tighter still.

Suddenly Weed was not alone in the stairwell and this enactment of a mugging without muggers was attracting some attention. People must not see the hand: they would think him strange. So he hid his hand in his pocket and headed on for the bus stop with his free, sane hand in his mouth.

He headed for the bus stop to go to work with a living personless hand in his pocket not because he thought Ms. Wap might like to see it, nor because he thought it could help him out in his duties, but because he was in too much of a state of shock to pause and take it in — and because he was terrified of missing time from work again.

Once on the bus, he did have the chance to pause and run through his options. His options went like this: He could go to the police and be clanged in the cells on the assumption he was a diabolical murderer, or just taking diabolical liberties. He could have remained at home with both the hand and the insane mirror ticking off the individual items of his sanity as they fled. He might reveal his dilemma to Ms. Wap at work. He might get sympathy for the trauma and the unfairness of having an animated severed limb inexplicably in his pocket, but he knew that Ms. Wap would simply disapprove of him being different yet again. His remaining option was ending it all with a messy, self-imposed death by drowning in the canal — and that sounded pretty good.

As he sat on the bus trundling slowly from one set of traffic lights stuck on red to the next, he began to reason that there must be a sensible explanation for the hand, and if there wasn't a sensible explanation, there must be an absurd explanation — but there must be an explanation.

Perhaps the hand had escaped from a film studio. Perhaps it was a mechanical wind-up hand. It was certainly winding him up. Or perhaps it was a digital computer-graphic hand, and perhaps even now the film crew were noticing that it was missing from the throat of the leading man and were organising search parties and gathering nets.

Talking of wind-ups, the thing could be a ghastly practical joke by Warren, like the time he hid a live ferret in the teapot or taped a knob of potassium under the rim of the toilet so that Weeds poo ended up on the wall when he flushed.

Or perhaps the hand was exactly what it appeared to be.

Then he looked at his watch and realised that his episode of panic had made him late and his brain seized up with fear again.

Ms. Wap was indeed curious as to how he could be late on so many occasions and how he could be late on two mornings in a row when he had been told very clearly time and again that the world would grind to halt on its axis and that all their dear and valued customers would give up buying air conditioners and start buying windows to open instead.

Weed had no particular reply. He stared at the floor tiles and arranged and rearranged his feet while Ms. Wap went through her full repertoire of questions that start with 'why'. When late for work, people can be very understanding if you have been kidnapped by aliens. It happens, you know. But sometimes the truth is better left in your overcoat pocket in the locker room so that it can escape and cease to be your problem.

The truth today was not so accommodating. The truth, in the shape of the disembodied hand, seemed to like Weed and was intent on accompanying him out into the field.

Out in the streets, it got quite excited. Perhaps it didn't normally get out too much. Weed would be half way through a pitch when he would find it escaping from the collar of his coat to scratch his ear. Or it would start running around in his trousers like a ferret. Or it would poke its fingers out of the spaces between the buttons in the front of his shirt. Once it gave the customer the thumbs up from Weed's flies.

Reports started flooding Daikon AirCon's main switchboard of an obscene three handed salesman on the loose.

When Weed's team came in at the end of the day they were greeted by Customer Satisfaction Enforcement agents wearing black suits and mirrored sunglasses who carefully counted the hands of each returning salesmanperson or saleswomanperson. They did not find the three-handed fiend that was wreaking havoc on their hugely expensive PR because, as luck would have it, the spare hand was sleeping curled up in the small of Weed's back.

Weed was worried: what if the hand woke up while the agents were checking him out? It might point the finger at him.

The agents and Weed's colleagues felt that this must be something to do with Weed. Among them, only Weed had a fully developed and independent personality and a keen and active sense of humour. His hair was also congenitally unkempt. All of which were definitions of unwholesome.

Weed survived the day, and back home in the evening, having fled back through his front door back into the sanctuary of his hovel, he hurled the hand into the pile of unwashed laundry on his kitchen/bathroom/living room/ bedroom floor and cowered in confusion and terror against the living room/bedroom/kitchen/bathroom wall.

In the tie mirror by the front door a well-groomed Weed watched on with a supercilious but otherwise inscrutable little smirk.

Eventually Weed un-cowered long enough to net the hand in a grey and rumpled work shirt and to knot it in the folds so it could not escape.

He left it there with the laundry. Well, where else would you keep an autonomous body part?

Exhausted, Weed planted himself in his futon. There was a pile of homework to do. He was in no condition to confront it. It was like asking a man just rescued from the desert to drink gravel. He resolved to get up at four to finish his work and slipped into coma.

He un-slipped from coma on the precise cusp of being on time or late for work. He cursed and dragged his shoes on ready for another wild flight to his place of humiliation and demoralisation. He tugged on his right shoe and toppled over. There was something in the shoe preventing him from getting his foot in. A misplaced kebab perhaps. It had happened before.

With a spoon and some more cursing he finally prised the impediment from the shoe. It was a foot. Weed screamed for the sake of consistency. Like the hand of the day before, it was warm and alive and where it terminated above the ankle there was a smooth cap of pink baby skin.

He scooped up the foot in a pair of old underpants and added it to the hand in the laundry pile. As if he didn't have enough to think about at work already, he now had a growing collection of body parts in his flat to get rid of. He looked hard at the liquidiser that his parents had made him buy and bolted for the door.

On his way out, the face in the mirror grinned at him.

At least that day he had a brief respite from the anxiety of stray hands appearing on his shoulder when talking to customers, but the respite was fleeting. The next morning he found a leg inhabiting his trousers and a respiring torso in his t-shirt drawer. That night there was an arm in his bed, a bottom in the undies drawer and he woke up with a foot in his mouth.

All the articles went swaddled in soiled linen into the laundry pile.

Weed was running out of clean clothes and this left him with a new dilemma: come laundry day, should he put this pile in the washing machine or give it a bath?

While he was wondering this, he was standing in front of his tie-checking mirror being futile with his knot.

His reflection since last night had given up any pretence of being a reflection and had taken to following Weed around the room with its eyes, wearing a consistently superior sneer and even leaning on the frame with an elbow. It seemed to have only one elbow. Weed wondered If it would like to make use of the spare elbow and arm in his laundry pile.

At this precise moment in Weed's ruminations the reflection leaned out of the mirror, grabbed him by the throat and butted him between the eyes. The reflection thing dragged the stunned Weed through the mirror frame and into the mirror then eased itself over the edge to drop onto the floor inside Weed's flat.

Inside the mirror Weed tried to staunch the blood flowing from his nose. He had no hanky so he used the broad end of his tie.

Weed's reflection inside the flat on the floor was an incomplete Weed. It was just head, shoulders, one arm, and a hand, which it used to drag itself laboriously across the mock parquet to the laundry pile, where it burrowed into the dirty clothes, grime stains and smells. There it flipped over and languished with a big, triumphant smile on its face.

It was a genially conspiratorial, pally kind of self-satisfied smile, and Weed was sure he had seen it somewhere before. It was a Daikon AirCon number one smile, the smile for people who were sure they wanted an air conditioner.

Until it turned its face back to Weed and it became momentarily the smile of the cat that had stolen the cream then evicted its owners from their home through a cunning and totally unfair legal trick, then won the lottery and married the owner's daughter. It was the kind of smile you wanted to punch whether it had just annexed your washing or not.

Weed was not a very punching sort of person, but he thought he ought to get out of the mirror and assert himself as king of his little castle, lord of the laundry pile, and all that, but for some reason he could not do so. The some reason being that the glass wouldn't let him. Funny that, if not actually odd. The glass hadn't prevented him getting in any more than it had prevented his reflection getting out. Thumping energetically on the glass now to escape was proving as effective as trying push over Mount Everest. As he remembered it through the blood and the pain, the glass had permitted Weed and his reflection to pass through with some supple buckling and an audible schloop.

Weed was wondering now whether there was something going on here that was beyond his control. There was indeed: his life was going on and completely beyond his control.

Perhaps his reflection had a key to open the glass, or a least a door handle. Perhaps there was some other trick to it, like there had to be another face within head butting distance for the trick to work. Or perhaps Warren really had spiked his crumpets with bad acid.

Weed is distracted from thoughts of escape by his reflection in the dirty clothes. Something is going on: there seems to be some kind of party, or some kind of frenzy, as socks and pants leap around as if the pile contained a school of starved piranhas. Or perhaps it is like an orgy and what perversion is here displayed! Unbridled passion at the contact of Weed's soiled smalls!

It soon becomes clear what perversion is being played out. His reflection has found the buried torso and they are wriggling together, twisting on their shiny caps of scar tissue. At the same time the legs and arms and feet are jiggling up against each other — acting out the words of the song, the ankle bone is connected to the shin bone, the thigh bone is connected to the naughty bone — until Weed's reflection and the assorted body parts have formed a whole: a lean, fit, trim, perfectly formed whole — quite unlike the original Weed in every respect except that it looks exactly like him.

What is the import of this bizarre event? Weed does not need to be told. This Franken-Weed, this doppel-Weed, this self-made-man-Weed, is on a mission to sell air conditioners and nothing will stop it.

Weed's interloper stood proud above the laundry, the same laundry that had abjectly failed to restrain this corruption of nature. The creature stood proud and naked above the laundry pile that had gestated it and given it birth without getting any cleaner. This monster stood proud on its laundry plinth of triumph ready to go out and take Weed's place in the world.

'Ah, ha!' thought the real Weed. 'Thwarted!' He was wearing the only clean set of clothes. The other Weed would have to do the laundry before going out and in that compact washer his parents had compelled him to buy that meant doing a sock at a time. The doppel-Weed would be there all day.

However, it seems that Weed's other has already thought that out. The doppel-Weed is as aware of the second law of thermodynamics as the original Weed. The second law of thermodynamics states that matter, or energy (same thing) left to its own devices will tend toward disorder. It is a strange law. Why hadn't Parliament formulated the law as matter left to its own devices would tend to increased order? Then the way to get the housework done or airplanes and bridges built would be to go away and watch telly or have a pint down the pub. However, the Parliamentary committee that had drafted the law had been leaned on heavily by the washing powder and kitchen cleanser lobby and the resulting law was designed to optimise their profits and not our living time.

The doppel-Weed knows that the way to reverse entropy is to supply energy. This increases the disorder elsewhere in the universe but hopefully not in your flat, but in someone else's down the street a way. Weed's fake-simile therefore decided to restore the local order by electrocuting the laundry pile by means of the toaster and a jug of water.

Mere moments later the clothes were glowing, gleaming, pressed and folded in a neat and only slightly smoking pile in the airing cupboard.

The reflection dressed, and preened in seconds — yet something was undone, something was missing. The reflection peered thoughtfully round the room until its eyes came to Weed in the mirror.

The thing approached, and Weed thought, now's my chance to butt the bugger, just as the bugger in question lunged through the mirror and started strangling him. Weed twisted and struggled but there was no loosening the tenacious, vice-like grasp. And suddenly the doppelganger let go, leaving its real self gasping and choking in the darkness behind the mirror.

When Weed peered again back into his room, he was met with the even, tie-adjusting gaze of his other, who had molded Weed's tatty old rag of a tie into a plump and pristine knot.

So that's what that was all about: that was no ordinary strangle, the reflection wanted Weed's tie, not his soul.

Ah, but in the corporate world, perhaps his tie is his soul. Weed hadn't thought of that!

The front door slammed emphatically and Weed was left alone, imprisoned in his tie-adjusting mirror.

Being the proactive get-ahead-get-a-hat, sort of dude he was, he did what any proactive get-ahead-get-a-hat sort of dude would do in the circumstances and blubbed and wailed all day, and deep into the night.

Eventually, the thing that had usurped his life and his laundry came bounding home did all the laundry, kebabed with apparent ease and relish, and plopped into bed for a brutally efficient short-but-regenerating kip.

The doppelganger, Weed noticed, did not do any work on the tachyon drive.

Weed noticed one other thing about his reflection as it curled up all cosy in Weed's bed: another of those punchable smiles. This one was not the haughty sneer of the victor, this was peaceful and oceanic, delighted and delirious, this was the smile of a baby who has been suckled and tickled at the same time; it was the smile of someone who has been lavishly praised by Ms. Wap. The fiend had actually sold an air conditioner.

Weed bided his time that night, trying to doze but not dozing. He propped himself against the mirror terrified of moving even a step away in the bright silver space of the mirror's interior.

He had a plan to escape. There had been plenty of time for planning while locked away and his plan was extravagantly good. He was going to wait for his doppel-

Weed to stop by the mirror to straighten its tie, then he was going to let it have it right between the eyes, just like the time he ended up being strangled.

OK, the plan lacked something. It lacked originality, it lacked shape, it lacked detail, and it lacked a chance of working, but it was Weed's plan, it was his only plan and he was going through with it. I mean, what else would you do incarcerated in slivers of glass and aluminium?

So he bided his time till morning. In truth it was not a long wait. His usurper, like Napoleon or Margaret Thatcher did not need a proper sleep. A few hours of kip that was so deep it didn't even register REM, and then like a mobile phone on its charger for a few hours, it was ready to go.

At the first stirrings of the usurper, Weed was alert and ready. He placed himself behind the glass in full head-butt readiness.

The doppel-Weed abluted, breakfasted and dressed. Weed was furious that this monster lingered to get the fried bread crisped just so. Weed had never cooked such a breakfast before work. For him breakfast came out of consumer-resistant plastic and was taken on the hoof.

To Weed's greater fury in his hyped state the doppel-Weed took an age choosing just the right tie for the day. Weed had nothing against looking good, but the reflection's care was perhaps excessive given that there was only one tie to choose from.

Eventually — too eventually — Weed's reflection came within range of the mirror. Weed coiled and tensed, his fingers rippled at the edge of the mirror's square. The doppel-Weed came closer and closer and stopped to tweak its tie before leaving.

Weed lunged head first at that smug supercilious grin he loathed so much and splatted his skull on the unyielding glass.

The doppel-Weed laughed heartily and straightened the mirror, which had been jolted askew by the impact.

Weed, still inside his prison trying to stem the hope that flowed from his nose, reflected that the biggest problem with his plan was now evident: it was complete bollocks.

So Weed slipped into his pulsating despair, eyes closed, forehead latched to the grease spot on the glass. And in this vacant and still state, he made mental contact with the doppel-Weed.

There was an audible whoosh and a blurring of space like in the movies and he was looking not at his flat through the window of the mirror, but looking through the doppel-Weed's eyes as it went about his — went about Weed's — business.

The doppel-Weed had beaten the morning crush and arrived early at Smiles House where he was psyching up for the morning's sales excursion with calisthenics while practising the four smiles — an activity for the real Weed akin to rubbing the top of your head and your belly and reciting Slavic tongue twisters simultaneously.

Wap strolled in and noticed the springing doppel-Weed.

'Early again, Bob. And getting in the mood.'

'Oh, I'm always in the mood,' said Weed with a big cheesy number one smile and a wink.

'Hmm,' said Wap very deliberately, 'Maybe you could sell me a thing or two.'

'Ah ha! A customer who knows exactly what she wants?'

'Well, maybe my air does need a bit of conditioning.'

'Then —'

'But I'm still undecided about the exact model. Options and after care are so important. But so is fit.'

Ms. Wap clicked away on those arch stilettos and the doppel-Weed emitted some silent yelps of primal psych and bounced higher still, while the real Weed wondered if there might be a bucket lurking in the mirror somewhere he could vomit in.

It was well known that Ms. Wap only had the hots for Stonewall. She was drawn to authority, strength and sales prowess. What was she doing chatting up Weed, even if it was an unprecedentedly groomed Weed? The prisoner of the tie-adjusting mirror was about to find out as he was dragged in his usurper's eyes out to the sales beat of the day.

The mini van of sales personnel stopped at a traffic light. The doppel-Weed opened the window and managed to sell a large wall-mounted installation to a passerby before the lights could change.

'Excuse me, sir.'

'Yes?'

'If you don't mind me asking, sir, do you have a family, sir?'

'Yes, I …'

'I imagine you want the best for your family, sir. Am I right, sir?'

'Yes, abso—'

'Does your family breath air, sir?'

'Yes, of …'

'And the air we breath is less than pristine and is a cause for concern for the family man who has growing and vulnerable children, sir. Would I be right, sir?'

'Well, yes …'

'And you would like your family to breathe wholesome air, sir, for the good of your family, sir.'

'Yes, I …'

'And would you like to have control over your environment to maximize the well-being of the family you love and who depend upon your strength and capacity to make important decisions in a trice, sir. Am I right, sir?'

'Yes!'

'And you absolutely want the best for your family, sir.'

'Yes!'

'Sign here, sir. Address. Phone number. Email address. Income — that's an exact figure, sir, not a range. Colour of wife's underpants … Thank you very much, sir, you have made the right decision.'

The minivan pulled away from the traffic light, the doppel-Weed got his sales chit stamped by the incredulous

Mr. Scourge and the real Weed was dragged through a day of interminable sales triumphs and fetid encounters with bored housewives.

The doppel-Weed had an unnerving sixth sense for which buttons to push to get sales. It was able to read fears and paranoias, vulnerabilities and vanities and work them until the victim became convinced that their only salvation was an air conditioner. It seized on muddles like a hungry and sociopathic cheetah on a lame fawn. It sold a fashionable young woman a nice little unit on the basis of her hearing hair conditioner for air conditioner.

All the while he amassed an embarrassingly thick sheaf of signed sales chits, more than most collected in a week of performance evaluations that would count towards commission, bonuses, pay rises, promotion and flutters from Ms. Wap's eyelashes.

Weed, and therefore his doppelganger, were not considered senior enough to work in the nice neighbourhoods, so many of his customers had no more pennies to rub together than Weed, yet his other would march into their lives, rearrange their budgets, figure out a nice HP plan that would have the families making easy, manageable payments for the next three generations; no matter that these were the straws that would condemn many to treading wheels in the debtor's prison.

Weed's pay next month would be chubby and healthy and pink and bouncing. In that, the doppel-Weed was ensuring he would not have to live like his customers.

It was the same with the housewives, all button pushing and rationalizing and wooing and quick exits. He had a schedule to keep.

At times the doppel-Weed had the women sign the purchase agreement at the peak of their passion, and he was out the door. Five minutes from the first push of the doorbell to fly-zippering exit — just the time the manual prescribed.

At the end, the real Weed was left shaking and weak-kneed, while his doppelself was strutting like an Italian striker.

The shift was over. Surely now it would come home and Weed would find a way through the glass to the beast's throat— or resign himself to eternal oblivion in the mirror, cut off from his life and the entire planet.

Yet, worse was to come. There was one thing that the real Weed had been keeping from his mind, but now the horror, like the tidal wave he was pretending not to notice or the wall of molten lava he didn't want to know about or the week-old stew in the saucepan he was ignoring, was upon him. The doppel-Weed was off, panting with anticipation, to Sam Smiles House to see Bobette — who screamed when she saw it.

'Bob — your hair! Your tie! Your eyes! What happened?'

'Do I look ruffled? I'm just a little windswept. Hectic day in the field. You don't set a pace like that and come out unsinged, you know.'

'Bob?'

'Ms. Wap's pretty darn pleased with me, I can tell you that.'

'You made a sale?' In her incredulity, the features of her face seemed to be making off in different directions.

'A sale? Thirty-six today. Thirty-one yesterday. Boy, there are some dimbos out there. You should have seen this one — dozy old cow. I got her to fit out her entire flat with a Zooper AA2010 system. It's designed for an actual entire office suite but she bought it anyway. Uses so much energy it needs its own power station — but the station is nuclear so it won't make any pollution, so that's all right. She and her family will be in hock for generations to come, if they don't freeze to death first.'

'Bob?'

'I like the way you call me Bob. It reminds me of — never mind.'

The doppel-Weed stepped very close to Bobette who said, 'Well, I have to call you Bob, don't I. It's your name. I'd look silly if I called you Sir Anthony Pipecleaner-Rump.'

The doppel-Weed was aghast. 'You mean, you —'

'It was a joke.'

The doppel-Weed paused, frowning to get its head around the joke. It didn't do very well and went back to its original line of thought.

'Your uniform, Bobette, why don't you put it on.'

The real Weed in his mirror banged on the glass trying to catch Bobette's attention. He yelled over and again, 'It's not me! Kick the bugger in the goolies and leg it!'

'I'm not on duty, it's past five. Why would I want to put it on? And I'm getting the oddest impression that I can see a little you in each of your eyes yelling and waving their fists.'

The doppel-Weed, unaware of the commotion behind its retinas, went on. 'And if you could carry a clipboard or a large file and count my sales chits very slowly while looking at me —'

'Bob?'

'— and cock your head to one side, just so.'

'Bob?'

'And tell me how you want me to sell you something, you know, the way — never mind.'

'Bob!'

'And while you change, I can watch.'

Bobette knew the real Weed wouldn't watch while she changed a light bulb so she picked up a handy ream of print out, said 'They've been getting to you again, haven't they. I could tell as soon as I saw your hair and tie.' And she hit him full force in the head with the paper. This was normally enough to bring a work-traumatised Weed to his senses. Today it caused him to sheer across the thorax and collapse in a pile of pieces on the floor. Bobette screamed and the real Weed tumbled through the mirror onto the floor of his flat. Without pause, he upped and fled to Bobette as fast as the number 23 bus would carry him.

When he arrived, the pieces of doppel-Weed still strew the floor and Bobette was still trembling and terrified.

At the sight of Weed she screamed again, picked up her trusty ream and thumped him in the side of the head.

'Ow! What's that for?'

'That's for that,' she said, pointing at the doppelremains. 'And for this,' she said pointing at the whole and apparently authentic Weed. 'I have never been so scared and confused in my life. What is going on?'

'I was — it was —' Weed tried to explain, but Bobette cut him off.

'How do I know you're real?'

'Erm, you hit me and I didn't —'

'Could be another trick. Reality is having problems today. She held her ream like a baseball bat, ready to let him have it at one false move.

'There's only one way to be sure. Put that tie on,' she commanded.

Weed obeyed, tugging the article from his dismantled other. In his hands, the tie turned immediately into willful red ferret on speed. When her boyfriend had finished making a complete pig's ear of this simple task and stood helpless with a clenched fist of a knot at his neck, Bobette dropped the ream and used the tie as a means to drag his head within kissing range.

'That's my Bob.'

Now Weed had his chance to explain, which he did, albeit in a slightly confusing rush.

'Hmm,' said Bobette. 'Acute self-disassociation disorder.'

'I didn't think it was cute at all,' objected Weed.

'What are we going to do with this?'

'There's only one thing for it,' said Weed with spine-tingling decisiveness.

They piled the doppelparts on a sheet and dragged them through the labyrinth of filing cabinets to the unused loo that had featured so prominently in the couple's first meeting. There they unloaded the bits one by one into a toilet pan, forcing each down the pipes with a bog brush.

'As soon as I saw him, I said he was round the bend,' quipped Weed.

Eventually, all that was left of the doppel-Weed was a sheaf of papers, a file and a biro, and all this too went the way of its late master.

Weed and Bobette embraced like two lovers who had given each other up for dead.

'There is one more thing I have to do before I am truly free of the curse of that thing,' announced Weed and promising to return as soon as his homework allowed he fled back to his little flat as fast as the number 23 bus would take him.

It was with considerable trepidation that Weed approached the tie-adjusting mirror. Would it contain another deranged alter-self? Would it swallow him up again? Would it extract some kind of revenge for the loss of the big child it birthed? Would it slice him into pieces and flush him down the toilet?

The mirror did none of these things. His reflection did what you would expect a regular, homey sort or reflection to do. It moved from side to side with Weed, bobbed up and down with him, pirouhetted with him, stuck two biros up its nose and sang 'Love Me Tender' with him.

Weed removed the mirror from the wall and put it in the kitchen sink where he beat it to pieces with the spanners he used for building his tachyon drive. Then he shoveled the bits into the food blender and ground them into a powder, which he then tipped them into an old biscuit tin — pausing only to eat all the old biscuits — and bound the tin with sticky tape. He then entombed the biscuit tin in a concrete-filled drum, which he hid in the back of his closet.

After tinkering happily with his spaceship engine invention for a couple of hours and generally reclaiming his life, he went to bed, got up bright and early feeling bright and early and got on a bus that was soon after dragged beneath the icy waters of Clapton Pond by a giant squid. Many of the passengers were drowned or eaten but Weed escaped unharmed — and covered head to toe in black squid ink.

When he came late into his training with his hair and his tie and his sheepishness and his smell of fish and stagnant ponds, Ms. Wap instantly knew the recent change had been reversed.

In the first break, she took him aside for his ritual reprimand, delivered in her resigned ritual tone. Weed beamed contentedly throughout. Compared to the horror of incarceration in the mirror, this dressing down was as familiar as a security blanket.

Ms. Wap broke off and searched frankly in his eyes for that bright sales star, that smooth callousness, that rugged indifference to everything thing else on the planet. Finding none of it she sighed, even more resigned than when she had started the lecture.

'Well. Bob. I don't know what happened but I know better than to ask.

'At four this afternoon I'll give you leave to go over to Auditing and Inaction to cash your sales chits. You must have quite a collection. I think you broke a few records there. Selling that high-power unit to that Eskimo was a stroke of genius. You may get an extra bonus just for that — which of course they'll take out of your salary as an incentive to earn another. You did get the chits signed by Mr. Scourge, didn't you.'

Ms. Wap spoke as if she knew this was the last time they would see a Weed sales chit. She spoke as if it were the end of an era and then Weed buried his face in his hands and laughed because he just remembered he had flushed all the chits down the toilet after his doppelthing without stopping to think what it was he was getting rid of.

Weed was terribly excited. It was early Friday evening, training was finished for the week and nothing else was scheduled for him by Daikon AirCon until the trainees' country excursion at six on Saturday morning when they would be bussed out of town and allowed to wander in the sun and amid the fields and trees and sell air conditioners to the locals.

When Ms. Wap wasn't listening, Weed had remarked that the sheep and the cows had suffered unfiltered air for quite long enough and it was nice to see Daikon AirCon doing something about it and that they might make good customers since they wouldn't be able to say no or close a door in your face. His colleagues looked a little startled and began asking him whether he really thought there was an agricultural market that remained so far untapped. This provoked a general discussion about the effect of conditioner-enhanced atmosphere on milk and meat yields and whether it would be necessary to roof and wall the fields or whether it would be adequate to have the animals huddle round one unit in the middle of the field.

Weed wasn't excited about the field trip. He was excited because Bobette was moving out of the office this evening. She was leaving her retreat, her sanctuary; she was moving back to the real world — or somewhere adjacent to it. She was moving out of the office and into his place. They would be able to drink tea together whenever they liked.

Their first meeting, while facilitated by a full bladder and a lack of attention to direction, had been mediated by tea. Tea quickly became matchmaker and enabler; tea was there every time they met.

Their tea drinking sessions had blossomed, had multiplied, had become a new and exciting way of life for them both. Occasionally, say once a week, they were actually able to enjoy one of these sessions together in the same room at the same time. Mostly they enjoyed their tea miles apart. Tea had come to symbolise their relationship. They drank tea to think of each other. They drank tea to be with each other. Tea washed away the dreary miles between them.

Some separated lovers would gaze upon the moon or the ocean and reflect that this was the same moon that looked down on their beloved, that this was the same ocean that lapped their beloved's toes half a world away, that the moon and the ocean bound them eternally no matter how far apart. Weed and Bobette gazed upon a mug of brew. And what gazing they got into! Casual observers might have assumed it was the tea itself that they planned to marry.

Bobette, free of the traces and whips of work or supervisors, curled like a cat around her tea while reclined on her bed of computer printout. She would drink slowly, reflectively and with slow relish, and then with her finger poke at the dregs to evoke her man's face. Weed would gulp rapidly any and every chance he got. He made a thermos every morning and drank it all before he even got to the bus stop. He couldn't pass a cafe without stopping for a fast one. He would ask his supervisor to be excused for the loo but would head straight for the vending machine in the hall and when he came back he would have to ask to be excused again because now he really needed to go. As a consequence of his excesses of tea, his teeth had become brown, his skin was turning yellow and his bowels were ruined. But the tea brought the two of them ever closer together.

As surely as marijuana leads to heroin the tea drinking led to heavier things, and Weed found himself blurting in Bobette's presence. Weed had had an unexpected afternoon off one Tuesday when their trainer was taken in to have a defective part replaced. He raced across town, his light heart propelling the lift to Bobette's floor without the normal aid of the winch. Bobette already had the kettle on.

'You look great in that kettle,' he said.

Around the third cup of tea when they were talking about the threat from global warming to the habitat of

Arctic moor wraiths and wondering about the effectiveness of Daikon AirCon's plans to build a huge global air conditioner system to reverse the warming trend, Weed did his blurting thing.

And here's the text of that blurt in full.

'Why don't you move in with me? Leave this place and we can drink tea together whenever we want. Or at least whenever we are at home together at the same time. It would be a base from which you could get back into the real world — if you want to because if you don't want to that's perfectly all right. Though in truth it would be considerably less comfortable than here and a lot colder too because after I've paid the mortgage every month there's isn't that much left over for utilities or food to be honest though we'd be OK for tea so long as we were two salaries and you could move on as soon as you were ready. Erm ...'

And Bobette had agreed by hurling herself across the room and landing right on top of him.

Now, this Friday evening, Weed stood impatiently outside the lifts on the ground floor, tapping his feet, tapping his fingers, and wishing there was a flight of stairs to Bobette's section so he could bound exuberantly up them, to arrive at the top becomingly flushed and puffed. But there were no stairs in sight. He had looked. This was a convenient building: movement was automated and the floors took you where you wanted to go. So he waited until a man in blue overalls came along and slapped a "Closed for Nonessential Maintenance" notice on the lift doors.

When eventually he got to Bobette's floor he felt something was not right. All looked fine but perhaps there was some subtle difference in the acoustics, or slight rearrangement of the light — that feeling we have all had when we get home and we know without looking that some intruder has broken in and helped him- or herself to some of the salami in the fridge without touching anything else.

He set off at top speed and with a lover's gait but soon found he hadn't found Bobette. The tight sprawl of desks and glaucomic clerks failed to cease sprawling, declined to give way to the steel grey walls of Bobette's sanctum. He walked, pushed, evaded, circumnavigated and jinked his way across the entire office floor without seeing a filing cabinet, a slipper or a chain of coloured paper clips.

Finally, he stood forlorn in front of the toilet she had first shown him to. Inside, the delicate paper snow had been cleared away. His footprints had been swept away with it. There was nothing left of either him or her in this part of the building.

Weed decided that he was on the wrong floor. This was ignoring the fact that he had passed Stonewall's cube to get here. It was so obvious: Stonewall's cubicle had been moved from the floor above or the floor below or two floors above or two floors below, fooling Weed into thinking he was on the right floor. This is what he told himself like a slowly unfolding mantra while running up and down the fire escape checking the floors progressively further from Bobette's.

Eventually, unbecomingly, sweatily flushed and puffed — when he found himself scouring the roof and the service yard out the back as if Bobette had been in either place all along and he had merely failed to notice the drizzle and the mangy cats — he had to face the disastrous truth: Bobette had been reorganised.

Now Weed made for personnel to inquire about Bobette.

'Can I help you?' asked the General Liaison Clerk, First Contact Group.

Weed explained he wanted to trace someone.

'Employee number?'

Weed gave his employee number and the clerk typed it into her computer. They waited a second for the computer to do its bit. The clerk had big, round cheeks — lots of big, round cheeks. Many of the cheeks were very large, indeed.

Some of them were inside her dress where they had slipped into a haphazard pile around her midriff.

The big, round cheeks on her face only needed some endearing freckles to set them off. Instead, they had some endearing pustules to set them off in the wrong direction.

Eventually she said, 'Robert D. Weed. Training. Revenue Acquisition. Section GAB/BS. Erm ... he was scheduled for a training but it was cancelled at the last minute. Funnily enough his security pass was registered entering this building not even an hour ago and he hasn't left yet. I wonder what he could want here. Hey, you might bump into him!'

The clerk thought that the prospect of such a collision was funny. So much so, in fact, she had to report it to her half-dozen colleagues.

'Hey, you might bump into him! I said!'

Her colleagues were quite baffled and silent until a tall, skinny bloke with whom she shared opticians and pustule cream, repeated the story for them.

'It turns out they're both in the same building only he didn't know it so she said to him "You might bump into him,"' This reformulation did the trick, and a whirlwind of hilarity engulfed their nest of desks.

When the General Liaison Clerks were finally all laughed out and they had dabbed the last of the tears from their cheeks, they got on their phones to spread the news throughout Daikon AirCon. Weed recaptured the attention of the clerk. He told her that he was the Robert D. Weed on her computer screen.

The clerk's face froze in a sort of wobbly O shape wondering where the upgrade of the humour was coming from. Her co-workers wondered too and halted in mid anecdote to listen.

'Your employee number? Are you lost? Your securicard number would have been enough. Why did you give me your employee number?'

Weed told the clerk that she hadn't specified whose employee number she had wanted, and anyway he was not lost, that Bobette Hope was lost, at least lost from him, though not necessarily lost from her own point of view.

'Someone else is lost? Well where is she?' asked the clerk quite disappointed that no more humour was emerging from this exchange and that Weed was quite clearly as daft as a monkey on stupid pills.

Weed reiterated that Bobette was not there and that was why he was asking personnel.

'Well, if she's not here how can I help her?'

'You can't. It's me who needs help.'

'You can say that again: you said you weren't lost and it was her who needed help, and now you're changing your story again saying it's you that's lost even though you're standing here in front of me plain for everyone to see, so how can you say you're lost?' The young woman's riveted colleagues had clearly sensed where the humour was coming from and going to, and the conversation was being relayed all over Daikon AirCon's phone system in real time, encrypted as a long stream of sniggers.

'I've lost her. I'm trying to find her.'

'Have you tried her desk? Her day-by-day schedule should be posted there.'

'I don't know where her desk is. She's been disorganised. I mean reorganised.'

The clerk's face was bobbling as if there were two cats fighting under the cushions: clearly it was Weed's oversight that had moved Bobette, and Weed was too comically dim to see it.

'First you say it's you who is lost and then you say it's someone else who's gone but it turns out it's just a desk you're missing. Try Office Services. Desks is more their line. People is ours.'

Weed imagined biting through her skull, and tried explaining again.

His clerk regarded him dubiously, and the bank of commentators behind her paused slack-jawed and in a state of suspended narration.

'All right, we'll try it your way. Employee number. The contactee's number.'

'I don't actually know.'

'Section designation nomenclature?'

'I, erm ... '

'You do know the missive recipient's name.'

'Hope!'

'I hope so too. This has been going on far too long.'

'No, that's her family name. Hope. Bobette Hope.'

'Bobette Hope? Is that a double-barrelled name? Is it hyphenated?'

Once Weed had explained, the clerk searched on Bobette's name and announced, 'That's it!'

Weed's heart leapt and fluttered and twittered behind his ribs like an Eed-up canary in a cage.

'Authorisation,' she went on. 'What's your authorisation?'

'?' inquired Weed.

'Who's looking for her?'

'I am!'

'You're not her line manager are you. You don't look like a line manger. Line managers have clothes and stuff, and, you know, an air of dignity about them.'

'No, I'm not her line manager.'

'Are you a proximate supervisor?'

'Er ... '

'A band three or above proxy?'

'A relative.'

'A relative?'

'Kind of. Absolutely.'

'Is there an emergency?'

'Kind of. Absolutely.'

'Yes?'

'I can't find her.'

'That's your emergency?'

'It's a catastrophe for me — for us — for me!'

'Do you have a validation certificate from a certified doctor or a practising emergency service?'

'We're supposed to be moving in with each other tonight. See, she's been living on the sixth floor here for months and months and doesn't have a proper home. That's one reason she was joining me at my place. That's why I have no way of contacting her except for here. And her me. I don't think she has my home phone number. Well, I don't have a phone.

'You mean this whole thing's personal?'

'Very.'

The clerk closed whatever computer file she was in with an emphatic stab and a clunk. The computer cackled gleefully. 'You see, without authorisation I can't do any more.'

'My authorisation is Slater Stonewall.'

'The clerk picked up the phone.'

'What are you doing?'

'Verifying authorisation. I'm calling Mr. Stonewall.'

'Don't do that!' squeaked Weed.

'Too late,' giggled the clerk.

With a wail unbecoming even a tortured dog, Weed fled.

Weed should have stood tall while the clerk called Stonewall. He should have then followed the clerk with stout dignity to Stonewall's cubicle to answer to the heinous crime of invoking the HND's name without the proper paperwork. He could have explained all to Stonewall and the clerk, and thereby all of Daikon AirCon would have seen the importance and justice of his position, might have fathomed the deep wells of passion sunk through him. They might then have stretched a point, located Ms. Hope and reunited the pixel-crossed lovers.

But it's funny how these things don't occur to us until it's too late. The French have a name for it: esprit de l'escalier. For Weed it was la revelation dans l'ascenseur qu'il avait fait quelque chose tout a fait bete et qui avait tout foutue — the revelation in the elevator that he had done something utterly barking, which screwed things totally — yet he was still carried by the same impulse that bore him from the office: a primitive and atavistic fear of pink slips, UB 40s, of being shown doors, of firings, of cannings, of letting goes and droppings; of sneers, superciliousnesses and patronisings; of imputations and denigrations; of bailiffs and evictions and slow deaths by starvation.

It's not that Weed was yellow; more that he was through-and-through green.

Downstairs, Weed skittered across the vast lobby, out the front door and right into the arms of a memory of Bobette.

The steps flowed like a majestic concrete tongue from the entrance of Perseverance House. Bobette approached them from the larynx with the same confidence as everybody else and gamely trotted down toward the street with Weed just a couple of paces behind.

Something spooked her. Perhaps it was the traffic, or maybe the crowds of people, or perhaps it was simply the sudden abundance of unadulterated sunlight that set her off, but her resolve evaporated like a vampire tricked out of its box at high noon and she abruptly switched into reverse, knocking Weed off his feet.

She maintained the same reverse trot, scattering startled suits and irritable couriers, until just before she slipped back into the reassuring dark of the throat where Weed caught up with her and scooped her gently back in a descending direction. Weed had his arm around her shoulder and cooed gently to her.

'Bob,' she asked in a very alarmed sort of way, 'why are you imitating a pigeon?'

'I'm not. I'm cooing gently to you. It's supposed to be very reassuring.'

'I don't wish to be mean, but please stop. It's actually quite scary. Uh-oh, here I go again.' She abruptly peeled away from Weed, cleverly sidestepping a clerk carrying a tower of file boxes with whom Weed was obliged to collide. Weed caught her at the same place at the top of the stairs, apologising abjectly to the clerk who was well out of earshot. On the next trip down, Bobette made a cross-body break which wrong-footed her man altogether, and used a slow and long procession of incense-swinging LAN engineers for cover until Weed crawled through some legs and dragged her down. There being no circus in town this week a large crowd was gathering, half of which was urging Weed on and the other half of which was wondering whether Bobette would like police assistance.

'We're perfectly all right,' they cheerfully shouted at their audience, and Bobette was up and running. Weed was all cued up this time and was right there to head her off at the first available turn and then again at the second. Bobette was forced to give up height to make room to jink or dodge or scurry or hurtle past her tenacious boyfriend, but he was always there when she turned to get back up the stairs and she was tactically compelled lower and lower until her feet were on the pavement.

This was Bobette's first trip outside Perseverance House in more than a year. Weed was trying to wean her back onto the real world. It was not very surprising she was on the edge of panic. The real world does weird things to lots of people.

On the pavement at the bottom of the steps, they found that some psychological barrier had been crossed and Bobette didn't try to bolt again. But it was only one barrier and the day was promising to be an emotional steeplechase. They were on their way down the street but Bobette was trying to hide in Weed's armpit.

Weed fumbled his sunglasses from his own face and poked them on to the panicking Bobette. They were big and funky even on Weed's skinnily elevated head, on Bobette's small round face they were two black dinner plates from one of the sillier lifestyle shops, yet they succeeded in calming her down — or at least succeeded in soothing the harder edges of her fear.

Under Weed's arm, Bobette whimpered 'tell me my name's not Gollum, tell me my name's not Gollum, tell me my name's not Gollum,' all the way to the underground station where the passage from sunlight back into enclosed spaces seemed to pacify her.

Weed and Bobette were going to the seaside. It was a trip down memory lane for Bobette and an entirely new experience for Weed. Weed had only ever been anywhere once in his life and he hadn't enjoyed it at all. That trip had happened to him only the week before and he still had his nose in a sling because of it.

Today they were going to have a picnic and build sand tower blocks on the beach. They were going to stroll along the seafront eating shellfish and chips, ride the big wheel and the roller coaster, they were going to have stewed tea and warm beer, they were going to paddle, wade, and swim. Weed wanted to go scuba diving and see a sunken wreck, or go down in a submarine and maybe do battle with a giant squid. Bobette said they would see what they could do.

And then there they were emerging from the railway station at the other end of their journey. It was a clear and beautiful day and the sky was a jaunty blue beret on the sea and the land, and Bobette was singing 'Whistling in the Dark' to reassure herself.

Weed and Bobette wasted no time in strolling up the prom at a leisurely pace, hand in hand, looking for a nice spot to have their picnic. The seafront sang and clanged and chinged and guffawed at them. Bobette said the place hadn't changed much since she was a kid. There was now a skate-through burger joint cum first aid station for the roller bladers. That wasn't there when she was a kid. Then there was the big wheel, which was mostly underground because of building restrictions on height. That was new. The arcades were full of VR games in which you could experience being somewhere other than the place you had come all this way to be. That was a little different from the old arcades but deleterious to the exercise of imagination

— when Bobette was a kid she and her chums had spent many happy hours hanging around in the arcades imagining the machines doing something interesting. One enterprising shop was exploring the appeal of sandy chips and mussels by doing away with the food and just selling plates of sand flavoured with salt and vinegar.

One feature of the traditional seafront remained: the laughing wotsit in the glass tank. Sometimes the wotsit would be a big jolly sailor or a pirate. In this case it was a big jolly laughing policeman built like a pile of balls, floor cushions, and inner tubes, splitting his sides to his own theme song. The sight of it arrested Weed. He was transfixed, and horror lashed his brow.

'I know when you're a kid those things can be pretty scary the first time you see one, Bob, but I didn't think they would strike adults the same way. C'mon, it's just plastic and transistors.'

'It's ... just horrible,' whispered Weed.

'Oh look,' said Bobette, 'I think I just saw a coelacanth.'

'Uh? Where?' exclaimed Weed.

They strolled on. They were happier than the town.

Down on the beach, Weed and Bobette laid out their picnic. First they spread out their mock-gingham plastic sheet and spread themselves on top of that. Then they opened up their little trove — their mock-wicker hamper — and spread out the food. We are often warned not to leave food out in direct sunlight or expose it to the air. In this unshaded spot the food was getting the full blast of UV and the sea breeze. The pale celery thrashed helplessly on its paper plate, the tomatoes scuttled for cover, the air pockets in the bread burst and the loaf deflated with a dejected sigh, the legs of chicken dragged themselves off the gingham to splash sand on themselves like mutilated crabs digging retreats. Only the mayonnaise seemed happy. It bubbled ecstatically in its jar and rattled its lid.

Bobette said 'It's important to eat correctly.'

'I do so agree,' agreed Weed. 'I'm a great fan of eating correctly. I generally start by putting the food in my mouth and then I chew it. I chew to the left and I chew to the right and I generally mash it all up and squelch it all about. It's the only way for me, really. Though I know it isn't so straightforward for some people. There are people who can't put it in their mouth to begin with, or ick it all up as soon as it's gone down, and the whole eating business is just a nightmare for them. There are some who can't get it down without the aid of oak panels, distinguished table mates, and oodles of wine, who can't digest anything that hasn't first been in the mouth of a dog. I know there are some that take their nourishment intravenously or by osmosis. Then there are those who swallow it whole or throw it over their shoulder or just smear it over their face because they think a face full of food makes them look cute. And there are those who simply can't get any and starve to death.

'But I'm not like any of them. I just bung it in my mouth and just, well ... eat it.'

'Correct eating,' continued Bobette, 'as in consuming a proper balance of fresh and nutritious, unadulterated, unprocessed foods that have their original DNA, foods that haven't been sprayed, injected or nuked, is of fundamental importance to an individual's health and well-being, and through the good farming practices such wholesome food requires, it is good for the general health of the planet.'

In truth, Bobette was still very disappointed that in three whole supermarkets she hadn't able to find anything that was fresh, nutritious, unadulterated and unprocessed, nor anything that had its original DNA and hadn't been sprayed, injected or nuked.

'Proper eating protects one against disease, reduces stress, improves longevity, and tastes good. It has been demonstrated that proper eating reduces violent and antisocial behaviour and increases intellectual thing. Performance. And proper eating generally spruces and buffs your well-being. Or did I already say that?'

In the end, Bobette and Weed had bought in the last chance supermarket a variety of packets and odds and ends chosen for their association with healthy things.

'Modern industrial food causes cancer, diabetes, heart disease, and a host of other debilitations. The production processes cause environmental pollution, degrade the nutritional quality of the food, are expensive in non-renewable energy, and all the food ends up tasting the same. And it's all sold to us as something better than nature could achieve, or, more insidiously, sold to us as nature's finest and best. I mean, look at this: ready-to-eat PermaBroc. The name made me think of broccoli grown by the organic permaculture method, but it is in fact broccoli that had been boiled down and reconstituted to look like and do the same thing as ... broccoli. Permanent broccoli, perhaps, since it'll never go off. Why did we buy this, Bob?'

'It was green,' said Weed dreamily. He was gazingly adoringly at Bobette. 'I love it when you talk like that.'

He touched her lightly on the cheek. 'Would you like a cheesy knob?'

'I beg your pardon?' worried Bobette.

'A cheesy knob,' explained Weed, brandishing a dayglo orange packet at Bobette.

'Oh, a Cheezi Nob!' exclaimed Bobette with some relief. 'I thought you ... Well, let's try one anyway.'

'Hmm,' said Weed taking one on a tour of his taste buds. 'The cheesiest part of them is their name.'

'Yes, they seem to be made of polystyrene,' Bobette observed.

'Interesting colour,' remarked Weed holding one up in the sunlight to see just how bright the knob's colour could become.'

'It could be a little yellower.'

'Not without blinding people.'

'Reminds me very much of that corporation yellow paint the city used to cover everything with before they switched to corporation orange.'

'Hmm, the city must have had a lot of that yellow left over. I wonder what they did with it all.'

Aside from reminding him of the corporation yellow paint, the colour reminded him very much of the one other time he had been on a trip. He hadn't enjoyed that trip nearly as much as he was enjoying this. In fact, enjoyment was something the whole trip had seemed opposed to.

Weed was in the countryside. It was a beautiful day. He languished on his back and contemplated the white daubs on the pristine blue glaze of space's bowl, he studied and marvelled at the casual filigree of the woods and reserved an ear for the jazzy warbling of the birds. He was fascinated that the trees were all propped up by sunbeams. He contemplated and marvelled as best he could through the puddles of yellow paint on the lenses of his goggles.

Another paint ball thudded into his chest.

Weed was laying on his back at the bottom of a ditch. The ditch was full of brambles and weeds, and probably full of rats and leeches and crawly things that bite. Weed was on a paintball outing organised for the Joyful Encounters trainees by Daikon AirCon. Paintball outings are designed to boost employee camaraderie, develop initiative and encourage competitive instincts. This was to be achieved by playing war. Weed had observed that if playing war developed initiative and competitive instincts, seven-year-old boys would be running the world. Ms. Wap pointed out to him that most elder statesmen had been seven-year-old boys at some point in their life, and indeed retained — cherished even — the characteristics of seven-year-old boys. Weed wondered further that if playing war was so effective, then real war would be much better practice than pretend war, and if shooting each other was good for competition wouldn't shooting their main competitors at ConAir Kondai be even better?

Ms. Wap reminded him that Daikon AirCon was contributing positively to world peace and harmony in a focussed and effective manner, and that Daikon AirCon would never go to war with ConAir Kondai under any circumstances whatever, unless Kondai breached the thirty-three point three percent partition of market share as laid down in the Geneva Air Conditioner Accords.

The trainees were packed on buses after work on a Saturday and driven to an army base whose facilities Daikon had bought, and which they maintained under an outsourcing agreement with the military. Although they would be fitted out with fatigues at a generous weekend rate once there, the trainees had taken the chance to do a bit of shopping of their own in the Army and Navy. Olive drab, khaki and camouflage, peaked caps, pouches, webbing, straps and buckles were de rigeur. Weed wore his sackcloth black suit because he didn't have any other clothes. Neither would it have occurred to him to change for something that was essentially work.

The trainees lounged with studied professional ease and a couple of keen young men kept to themselves on the back seat practicing their thousand-yard stares and drooling a little.

Ms. Wap chatted amiably about scroll compressors and rotas, and made careful notes in her training log about her charges on the bus.

At the army base there was a night of smuggled-in drinks, screaming, and running backwards and forwards between the men's and the women's dorms. There were pillow fights, the amusement of filling beds with talcum powder, billiard balls or tampons — and in Weed's case, nails and sump oil.

They were roused at five in the dawn by a raucous Ms. Wap who had donned the red flashes of regimental sergeant major drag for the occasion and had even pencilled herself a small moustache with eyeliner.

They were doubled into the Daikon canteen and ordered to buy a huge and sustaining breakfast. Everybody cracked a joke about last breakfasts and then about last shags, and they were doubled outside before they could finish eating to be drawn up in ranks on parade. They were issued paintball guns and goggles. A real sergeant major Daikon had acquired as part of its outsourcing agreement warned them the paint could be really messy if it got in their hair, and said they might want to wear hats or scarves. A few had already anticipated this and had brought along steel helmets.

Then there was training in the use of paint guns — apparently you had to point them where you wanted the ball of paint to go and pull the trigger. There was training in combat tactics — you were supposed to run, shoot, and then run again, though shooting, running and shooting was an option when you had found your confidence with the basic moves. The sergeant major also trained them in frightening snarls and blood-curdling screams, as essential for a soldier as a rifle and a good pair of boots.

'You there with the hair,' bawled the sergeant major at Weed. 'Why are you smiling? You look like you're in the sweet shop, not the battlefield.'

'I'm not smiling, I'm snarling,' said Weed.

'You will address me as sir before and after you speak, you frilly doily,' screamed the aptly titled SM.

'Sir, I'm not smiling, I'm snarling, sir.'

'Don't contradict me, you piece of needlepoint. That's a smile, not a snarl! I've been in the army since before you were wet behind the ears, since before you were born, since before your molecules were grubbing around in the primordial dung, and I know a snarl when I see one, and I'm not seeing one now. I'm seeing a big poo eater's grin. Do you understand me? You are not selling girls' blouses to the enemy here, you are selling them death, you are about to wrench out their hearts with your bare hands so that the last thing they see with their dying breath is you feasting on their living entrails!

'Now snarl! Take it from me, smiling does nothing for killing. It doesn't put people off killing you. And then they murder you. I think you'll find that holds true of most conflicts, you flower arrangement, you.'

'Si — '

'Listen to me, you delicate little cucumber sandwich, do you have many enemies?'

His colleagues nodded vigorously.

'Si — ' Weed wanted to shake his head, but wondered whether a nonverbal communication should be prefaced and suffixed with "sir", or some kind of respectful gesture such as a bow or a kiss.

'You'll find that people who snarl don't have a lot of enemies. And when you don't have a lot of enemies, the world seems a much brighter place. When we snarl we make other people scared and when they die of fright still more people get scared. Snarls are exponential, you Jane Austen novel, you. Do you know what exponential means? It means something gets bigger quicker than you would expect. And when eventually everybody in the world is snarling and all their enemies are lying on their backs with their legs in the air, there'll be no more wars and we'll all be wondering why we ever bothered to smile. In this way snarling is making a unique and meaningful contribution to world peace and harmony and understanding between races because we have scared people to death on all known continents.

'Our snarls have been developed in that most human of environments: the battlefield. Our snarls have been created and tested for your convenience you ungrateful pile of scones. Snarling is one of the most natural and simplest of human activities. They're meant to help you. We just want you to be frightening.

'Now, does anyone have some bog paper so this big chintz curtain can wipe that crap off his face?'

If Warren had been there to witness Weed's humiliation he may have renamed the sergeant major Onan the Barbarian. Weed was made of more charitable stuff and merely wished for invisibility or death.

Eventually the trainees were divided into two teams, the black team and the white team. Ms. Wap wasn't going to let crass symbolism go: black is a negative colour, the colour of failure, despondency and underachievement. This labelling of her beloved trainees could cause irreparable damage to their self esteem, and those on the white team might even try to start thinking for themselves. Before she can say anything to the sergeant major, however, some of the lads on the white team piped up.

'White? No way are we virgins! Just you ask my mate. Why do we have to be the white team?'

The sergeant major was able to understand and restrained himself from suggesting a white team and a pink team. After chewing his tongue for a while he suggested a red team and a blue team. This was great with the boys from white who were now blue but provoked outrage from the red team over the political symbolism. They raised voices at each other until they settled on tagging the teams navy blue and dark blue respectively over the sergeant major's reservations about explicit reference to poofters.

The two teams then deployed to their starting lines in the woods. Their objectives were to find each other's HQ — a hanky tied to a stick — and steal it. The quickest thieves were the winners.

Weed was told to stand far out on the left of his team. His job was to foil any attempt to outflank them by ambushing the ambushers. If there was no ambush, he was to work his way behind the opposition line and cause havoc in their rear by disrupting their strategic lines of communication.

The combatees advanced in extended line toward each other. They had all the combat moves: all the prowls and the stalks, the slow pirouettes, the lithe bounds from tree to tree; they held their paint guns two-handed and at arm's length or poised near their ears. They had all the moves because they had seen them on the telly, and the SM would have been most impressed if their moves had been anything to do with actual military procedure.

Eventually, the two teams met. They regarded each other across the thirty metres of dried twigs, cones, exotic fungi, and crisp wrappers that had suddenly become no man's land. Then without word or signal, they surged forward and joined together to create a new line, which wheeled about and went off in search of Weed.

Finding Weed was not the simple matter it should have been. He was not on the left flank where his team had put him. Weed was lost.

Weed was thinking this left flank gig was great. The early morning air was beautiful and fresh and stimulating. The sharp air was scrubbing out his alveoli and picking clean his pores while the sun winked affectionately at him through the branches of the trees.

He wedged his gun in his armpit and his hands in his pockets. He drifted a little further left to enjoy the quiet and the peace that seemed to be hanging around there and shifted gear into full saunter.

He kept his eyes peeled for an ambush. If he saw one he would walk right into it. If he was shot early in the game, he could stretch out on a log and just get into being there. He contemplated shooting himself in the foot, but worried Ms. Wap might realise the splat was self-inflicted, and that he would find himself in a court martial.

Crunching through the withered hands and smoked bones of the wood, he might have mistaken his colleagues, as they flitted between the trees, for naiads, elves, or flibbertigibbets. However, in his reverie he noticed nothing until his colleagues had spread their net and the first paint ball smacked into the back of his head. Before he had time to register what had hit him, a second cracked into his right ear, and a third exploded painfully on his right cheek. Then the balls were whacking and thudding into him all over like speeding, kamikaze wasps.

He tried to cover himself with his arms, but there was too much of him to protect, so he started running, but the others were whooping and leaping and seemed to be coming out of the woods from all directions. He tried spinning and stumbling and falling over logs, but this caused him to plunge into a ditch. Wedged and snared in the bottom, he had no way of hiding from the yellow barrage.

Now there was no chasing to do, the gunmenpersons of Joyful Encounters lined up either side of the ditch and emptied their weapons on him — fire, reload, fire, reload, fire, reload. They had each been issued with fifty rounds of paint so Weed's murder took quite a long time but the rain eased up eventually, and stopped even more eventually. Hollering and hooting, the clouds parted and drifted with the prevailing mood toward the bar.

Weed considered staying just where he was in the ditch. He couldn't see much point in moving. He contemplated the world in yellow through yellow-stained goggles, and thought it wasn't quite as good as it was unyellow, though the yellow did have its own appeal — it appealed in that it was yellow, which is a nice enough colour on its own. However, the yellow's appeal was diminished because it was all over his view of the woods and clashed with the colours and the shapes there. It was a sort of contextual and contingent disapproval of yellow. He couldn't think of anything nice to say about the yellow in his mouth though. There the context was all uncontingent and foul.

He thought of staying just where he was, he thought of putting down roots and raising branches and leaves and of just growing, of just being a shrub and of not being a salesmanperson or an employee or son or human being. He thought of just being.

He thought of Bobette and unwedged himself from the bottom of the ditch.

Once he found a section of ditch bank shallow enough to scale, he paused to smear about the yellow paint on his tunic with a dock leaf. He felt guilty about besmirching the leaf, resolutely dangled his head from his shoulders and trudged back to the little white herd of Nissen huts where they had spent the night. He couldn't bear the thought of being cooped in the bus with his colleagues for the journey back and wondered whether the driver would permit him to ride under the floor with the luggage.

Finally back at the camp, he saw there were buses already waiting and he was swept up in a flux of camouflage and deposited on a seat. When the bus didn't take him back to the city, and when he was put on a charge for forgetting his rifle and for being painted yellow while on red alert, he realised he had boarded the wrong coach. His NCOs were unable believe that he was a civilian and was on the bus by mistake. Nobody could be that stupid. Not even an air conditioner salesman. They assumed he was a newbie who couldn't take the pace and was working on a discharge for psychological malfunction. By the time the commanders worked out they really did have a weed in their patch, they were already on a military transport plane winging their way to another corner of the continent, to a region not blessed with the peace, plenty, air conditioners, or great tv of Weed's homeland, and where people were trying energetically to kill each other.

This contingent of infantry that now included Weed was attached to a heavily armed, technologically superior, multi-national force assigned to enter the country and stand by and watch impotently while the locals murdered, looted, raped and pillaged each other.

Weed's commander decided that he wouldn't shoot Weed on the spot, but that once they had landed, he was obliged by military regulations and the Geneva convention to detain him and lash him to a lamp post in Sniper's Alley until they could fly his remains out.

However, Weed and his irritating, non-regulation hue were quickly forgotten. As the transport touched down the war turned very inclement indeed. There was a hail of small arms fire, a sleet of mortar shells, a downpour of artillery, gales of concussion, tornadoes of fire, tsunamis of smoke and debris, and a general, all-over earthquake.

All the neighbouring militias and factions had decided spontaneously and simultaneously that what they really needed was an airfield, even though they had no planes and were too busy with the conflict to consider flying away for a holiday. They were descending on the airfield in great numbers and quite oblivious to or uncaring about the people already there. After all, if it was peace the peacekeepers wanted, they should go away somewhere peaceful like the Seychelles or Marbella. Peace just wasn't a happening in these parts; peace was not a thing around here.

Weed and the troops were already down the ramp and on the tarmac and there was no going back. Some hedgehog instinct had Weed curl up on the ground and cower. Honed military instinct had the others zigzagging through the maelstrom to bunkers Weed couldn't see, where they could cower professionally in comfort and safety.

Buffeted like a tumbleweed in a hot desert wind, Weed eventually rolled to the airport perimeter, through the tattered and shredded chintz of the chain link fence and on into a leafy and pocked suburb; he rolled through the gardens and their gardenias and slit trenches, ornamental ponds and craters, swings and trip wires, gnomes and claymores, bird boxes and machine gun nests, trikes and lost feet. Weed rolled under and by the guns of the combatants, but because of his yellow colour and yellow demeanour, nobody bothered to take a shot at him.

Finally, beyond the suburbs, he came to rest. It was a beautiful day. He languished on his back and contemplated the big blue O of the sky, which was sucking smoke from the trees and the nearby farmhouse, he marvelled at the demented filigree of the flames eating the barn and the plough, reserved an ear for the inane twatter of the guns and the screams of the children, and was fascinated that these big men with rifles seemed to be propped up by sunbeams.

Weed was wedged in another ditch. Along with the rodents and leeches and crawly biting things, the ditch contained anti personnel mines, razor wire, and a skull. He didn't want to put down roots here, so he unwedged himself and peered over the lip like a rabbit that has tunnelled into the dog pound.

The ditch runs alongside a dirt road that decants into a farmyard. On the other side of the ditch are woods, bolt-straight beech trees in a froth of bracken and small bushes. Weed must have come through the woods to get here, and a sensible Weed would return that way as fast as it could tumble. But the Weed pauses a moment, horrified and captivated by what is happening in the farm. He has seen this all before on tv and in films, but now it is happening here in God's Own Panavision and Sensurround and it's not quite the same thing.

Men with guns are on the farm and they have with them a lot of terrified people who have no guns: several families gathered from the adjacent cottages and small holdings. Some of the civilians are arguing with the gunmen, others are hugging the children as if the hugs would keep off the bullets and the rifle butts. The gunmen are big and burly in their fatigues but when undressed and in the bath they are probably as skinny and deformed as Weed and all the commuters we see daily.

The gunmen have separated the local men from the women and the kids, and are leading them away from their families up a rough track that threads from the farm and into the woods near Weed. The captives are either very old or very young, wrinklies or just teenagers, but a couple are in between, in their thirties or forties. They are probably husbands to some of the women left behind. And because they are not with their own army, they must have made the decision that fighting is not for them. But the decisions we make in our life are quite irrelevant when bigger and more important people think they have bigger and more important decisions to make on our behalf.

The paramilitaries do not make it clear what will happen to the men. This makes the situation more frightening: it is like a big Russian roulette. Will they be shot, will they be imprisoned, will they be put to work, or will they simply be let go? It is the hope that is difficult to deal with, and the gunmen were playing with hope; feeding it and dashing it; waving it around then putting it away again. In despair we fight or give up. In hope we do neither, we become pliant, we just go where we are put and do what we are told in the belief that this might keep us alive. Hope evokes pain because it might be false hope; it evokes pain because it makes us aware of how unnecessary and cruel and deliberate our suffering is.

In war everything is turned on its head. Even hope is conscripted to become a weapon.

The men with the guns represented the ethnic — and therefore the moral — majority around here. The families without the guns represented the moral minority, and as the smaller community they clearly posed a great threat to the racial and cultural integrity and identity of the greater group. They were also just cluttering the place up. To the majority, this minority must have looked like weeds in the garden, slugs in the salad, honest DNA in a tomato, a lump in your mash, nutrition in your pot noodle, spinach on your plate; with these guys around, the community was unpasteurised, unhomogenised. They had to be organised, cleaned up, straightened out.

The apparent leader of the irregulars was a young fellow, not much different in age from Weed. He had an adolescent face and his hair was immaculately combed and clinically parted at the side. The hair lay obediently in serried ranks and waves on his scalp — perhaps his hair was obedient because it too was scared of men with guns. He could have been one of Weed's co-trainees. On a train in Weed's home city at eight in the morning nobody would have given him a second glance but for his assault rifle, bandoliers and festoons of scalps and panties on his webbing.

This nice young man now picked out a woman from the crowd of families and dragged her a little way from the group. Her two children one about three or four, the other about two followed her. They were frightened and screaming. The woman was angry, frightened and screaming. He had pulled her from the larger group because he needed some elbowroom, which he used to slap her once over the head. Then he used the same elbowroom to menace the children with his gun.

The separated men had not yet disappeared into the woods and the woman's husband quite unreasonably decided to object to his family's mistreatment. He tried to run back to his wife's aid, but two of the guards blocked him and tried to bounce him back into line. This didn't stop him shouting and hurling abuse and his own orders at the chief, who paused in his beating to look irritable and interrupted. The husband's friends were now trying to pull him away. There was nothing anyone could do.

The top gun broke off from beating and terrorising the woman to trudge across the clearing to the husbands and fathers, eyes indifferently on the ground all the way, as if plodding back to close a gate he'd had accidentally left open. When he arrived in front of the angry, remonstrating husband he looked up just long enough to raise his rifle and shoot him once through the head.

The gunman waved his arms at the surviving men and his underlings urging them to get moving as if encouraging herd of dozy school kids to get back to the classroom at the end of break or as if shooing geese in the park. Then he trudged back to the women and children without even a glance at the corpse.

The village men moved on without further fight or protest. At last there was some certainty for them in the situation: arguing got you dead.

Weed had never seen a person die before and he wondered about an appropriate reaction. He considered vomiting. He thought of screaming but didn't want to give himself away. He wanted to flap his arms and run up and down the length of the ditch like a headless chicken but didn't want to get his head blown off by an antipersonnel mine. He eventually reacted to the murder by becoming paralysed. A tape loop started up in his head, a tape loop that replayed the murder over and over again, and would continue replaying the murder for all the short life time left to him.

The most terrifying aspects were not the raw fact of death or the capacity to take life, although they were quite sufficiently terrifying on their own, thank you very much. Weed's terror was compounded by the unprefaced abruptness of the act, of a human transaction so fast and violent it left brains and bone spattered in the dirt. And the way the dead man just flopped. There was no Hollywood leap back into the bushes, or noble embrace of the earth, just this rag doll flop, as if all his ligaments had snapped at once, leaving him to pile on the floor, as if life had suddenly stepped sideways out of the body and gone off about its own business elsewhere. And there was the indifferent casualness with which the young man murdered: it was just another trivial task in the day's dull labour.

The boss, the chief, the fuehrer, the head baboon, returned to the more important business of brutalising the woman. Seeing her husband die had made her noisier and this was a good excuse to hit her about a bit more and throw in the odd kick.

When the other women moved to intervene, the guards pushed and dragged them back, and bought their silence by training their guns on the children. And all the while, these soldiers kept a conscientious watch on their leader and the object of his kicks and curses.

These men hadn't reacted like this when her husband had begun arguing. Then they had maintained the same impatient indifference shown by the boss: the atmosphere was different now; something other was happening. They were now very tense, their guns were raised and their eyes were quick.

The boss slapped and kicked some more, then tugged at the mother's blouse, ripping off a couple of buttons. One more slap and another yank to remove more buttons. It was very obvious to everyone that this is in rape what foreplay is in love making, and the man was getting himself very heated.

The kids clung to their mother and with tears and wails bargained for her release. They were getting in the way and their mother's tormentor made more space for himself by grabbing the elder's hair and twisting him away into the grasp of the nearest of his colleagues. He moved the toddler with the sole of his boot in one piston jab that hurled the infant to the ground. She lay gulping and red, too winded to cry, beyond the help of her pinned mother or penned aunts. Laying there, her brain, which understood only wanting or not wanting and playing or not playing, whose whole world was a small house with toys and nice parents in it, had not the slightest understanding of what was happening, of why she or her mother were hurting so, or why her father didn't come and help, or why he was still laying down after the cruel man shouted at him.

Weed leapt from the ditch and strode through the sun and the butterflies and the smoke, unholstering his paintball gun from the armpit of his fatigues. Intent on their violence, the bandits didn't notice Weed until his first pellet of yellow burst on the boss's shoulder blade. The boss turned slowly to see the uniformed and bright yellow Weed struggling with the breech on his air gun, trying to insert another round. He watched curiously while Weed took careful aim and shot him deliberately in the chest. He tested the yellow paint on his finger while Weed reloaded, and then before Weed could shoot a third time he took quick and careful aim at Weed's forehead and let go a single bullet.

Weed reeled over backwards and crashed back-of-the-head-first into the ground. The well-groomed tormentor strode over to check the intruder was dead. Weed's face was a mess of blood and grit. No need to waste another bullet here. He took the paintball gun and the remaining pellets, planning to give them to his children. He took the goggles for when he went back to work in the sawmill after the war. Turning back to the woman and children, he shouted that all the sluts and the bitches and the whores should take their vermin brood and get the hell out of there and never be seen again in his universe.

Some spell had been broken, some lust had been sated, some anticipation had been satisfied.

The gunman watched the women fleeing with a feeling akin to the warm but irksome afterglow of a premature ejaculation. Then he turned and bade his band follow him into the woods.

Weed was found two days later by two Daikon AirCon sales operatives who were in the country doing a bit of pre-post war networking and reconnoitring for reconstruction opportunities. They were feeling pretty good because they had just sold a pretty meaty air conditioning unit to a beautifully manicured militia man who was festooned with human scalps and female underwear and a pair of goggles.

They spotted Weed by a motorway cluttered with jams of rusted or burned cars, lorries, and military hardware. There were, of course, many lost souls in this hell of this warred upon country, and one more or less would have made no difference to the salesmen, but something made them stop. They say it takes a priest to know a priest; perhaps it was that instinct that recognised the fellow traveller, perhaps something of Weed's catatonia said "Daikon".

Weed was wandering dazed. He was covered with yellow paint and blood, and was minus the tip of his nose. Weed had survived when the tip of his nose hadn't by executing one of his farsighted lapses into unconsciousness the moment he saw the muzzle of the militia leader's gun. As he keeled over, the bullet had passed over him grabbing only the ultimate point of his proboscis as it went. When he awoke outside the farm he had no idea where he was. All he could see was the traumatic memory of flopping rag dolls and black eyes that hid death, and all he could hear was the crying of petrified children that had long since fled.

He was plucked from the roadway and shipped home, where he arrived with a huge field dressing taped to his face to discover a bill waiting for the loss of his paintball gun, and arrest warrants on charges of travelling with no documentation, and participation in unlawful paramilitary activities.

On the beach Weed and Bobette squinted suspiciously at the cadmium comestible Weed was holding up. But concentration is a fickle and flighty thing, and Weed's was led astray by the commotion in the surf on the other side of his fingertips, a commotion that was also thumping up and down the beach and thumping in circles around them. In truth, the commotion had been with them since they arrived on the prom, but it was their first outing together, they had both been under a lot of pressure at work, and their attention had thought it might spend some quality time with just Weed and Bobette here — and perhaps put on its old straw hat, and bask in the warmth of their mutually admiring gazes. But now its head had been turned and it was off, dragged around by the other events of the beach. Specifically, it had been hijacked by a large flotilla of rubber dinghies, row boats, rafts, and a one-sided riot.

An armada was coming ashore and along with it there was a tide of people who were not here for the candy floss. These people had left home without time to prepare for the beach. Instead of inflatable beach balls they carried balled bed rolls and bundled clothes; instead of a thermos of tea or a bottle of ale, they carried the oil they saved from tins of sardines because they had nothing else to eat; instead of chips they carried shrapnel in their backs and legs; instead of deck chairs they carried the memory of biers; instead of shooting up the bug-eyed monsters in the arcades they hoped never again to see the monstrosities they left behind, and hoped never again to be shot at.

These were displaced people, these were people who had been chased, gunned, burned and raped out of their homes. These were refugees. They were from another country, the country in which Weed's nose had been recently shot. They believed that Weed's country was supporting them in their plight, and even getting involved in their civil war to help them out, and they had jumped to the conclusion that this was a good place to escape to when things were getting too mad at home.

They were stumbling through the surf between the bathers, and scrambling across the sand through the beach lubbers, and while they were doing this, law enforcement officers of Group Security 4 Us — the company that had bought the policing franchise for this district — were compelling as many as they could catch into the backs of police buses and vans lined up along the promenade.

The police — in button-down visors and button-up flak jackets, behind button-shaped shields, and cheerily raising buttons on people's heads with batons — upended, grappled, and dragged the refugees; they blocked and tackled them, they tossed and turned them, doubled and nelsoned them into the backs of the waiting mariahs and paddy wagons.

The refugees assumed they had been dumped on another hostile shore by the people smugglers, or indeed dumped back where they came from. They didn't know whether to come quietly, sit on the beach and cry, make a bid for the hills, or swim back out to sea in the hope that the currents would be kind and drown them quickly.

So they ducked and weaved, or plodded and laboured through the cops and the sandcastles and the picnics, until either they cleared the promenade and disappeared in the streets behind, or until they were scooped up and shovelled away.

'The cops are sponsored by Daikon AirCon in this area. You can see the smiley breeze logo on their truncheons,' Bobette pointed out.

'So you can. Actually, under the terms of our contracts I believe we are supposed to make our presence known to them and offer assistance, because under the terms of their contract with the contractor, there aren't enough of them to do the job and, they aren't paid enough to be motivated to anything other than brutality.'

'But I think we might just sit here and have our day.'

'I think we might.'

Bobette grimaced at the Cheezi Nobs and emptied her mouth into a tissue. 'You know,' she said, scowling at the pasteurised, homogenised, ionised, vitamin boosted, genetically modified water she was using to swill out the knobby remains, 'I am going to say something that will seem very unlikely and possibly in bad taste. There is a relationship between these refugees and these Cheezi Nobs.

'Men are on a mission to dismantle the world and put it back together in a different order. It's not like the world needs re-ordering, it's men's way of asserting themselves over it, of possessing it. A dog will pee on a lamp post to mark its territory. A man will demolish the lamp post and erect a new one its place.

'Food isn't food until men have taken it apart, until it has been processed and reconstituted. A nation isn't a nation until you've terrorised or murdered or raped someone who is a bit different, until you've eliminated anything you can't control from your space.

'A river isn't a river until you've defined its course with concrete. A thought isn't a thought until it has been written out for you and has a stamp of approval on it. Air isn't air until it has been forced into a scroll compressor and then squirted back out. Freedom isn't freedom until it has been sanctioned at the highest level. Life isn't life until it has been squeezed dry.

'You pull up weeds and then poison the ground so nothing can grow.

'In all cases, whatever you rearrange, whatever you re-make, you leave it less than it was before — and often times, like kids, you can't even put it back together in any working order.'

'Me?' asked Weed pathetically. He was not sure he personally was responsible for all the iniquities on the planet. He was responsible for the iniquity of bad salesmanship and getting things idiotically and inexcusably wrong but surely not all the other things.

Well, if he was complicit, he was going to defend his corner.

'One thing about the control junkies, they do have a few uses. They taught me how to smile, for example.'

Weed flashed Bobette a dazzling number one. Nearby, a child burst into tears.

'Yuck! That is grotesque! What did you do that for?' asked Bobette. The child's parents were muttering darkly.

'That was a Daikon smile,' Weed mumbled apologetically. It was the first time he had provoked that kind of reaction from Bobette, and deep inside a lower lip was trembling.

'See what I mean? Even a smile isn't a smile until it has been prised off your face and nailed back on upside down.'

An airliner screamed low overhead picking up a cloud of sand, chips and towels in its slipstream.

'Fascinating,' observed Weed, raising an eyebrow. 'The frequency of the yellow in the food colouring has confused the navigation system of that jet.'

'Well put it away quickly before you bring another down here.'

Weed popped the munchy in his mouth.

'Not there!' warned Bobette urgently, and Weed popped it back out of his mouth with sufficient startled velocity for it to travel several metres and ping audibly on the skull of a refugee who was struggling up the beach with her worldly possessions under one arm, and two howling children under the other. She dropped to the ground with a despairing scream.

In the previous few days she had seen her husband shot to death, had fled her home under the muzzle of the same gun, had been beaten up and nearly raped, had been robbed blind by people she paid to help her, and now, in this supposed sanctuary, she had been shot in the head. She pressed the sand- and snot-caked faces of her screaming children into the ground and below the bullets. She bled tears on them in farewell and entrusted their wellbeing to God, there being no other individual around she could ask for help. She prayed that the children — no more than toddlers — would not be defiled, tortured, beaten, or burned alive. She had seen these things happen to other children in the country she had just fled and had no reason to believe since being shot in the head that such brutality was not being practiced here too. She thought and said all things quickly before her life finished escaping from the hole in her skull.

'Oh, heck! Do you think I ought to go and apologise?' Weed set off through the flailing boots and bodies of the riot to say sorry.

He knelt over the exhausted woman, tried to help her and her kids to their feet. Even in the chaos and the fear, she recognised Weed as the man who had saved her from being raped by the human monster who had shot her husband back on their farm a few weeks previously. Here was the very man with the strange gun that shot symbolic yellow bullets who had died as he helped her. Who was he, what kind of demon, ghost, saint, or comic book character that appeared only in her darkest moments and was immune to death? Unaware that this was the very same person who had just fatally shot her with a Cheezi Nob, she pressed the kids into her saviour's arms.

The police, too, recognised this as rescue, but not the magical kind. They saw it as help from one illegal to another, because no sun lover would come to the beach in clothes as shabby as Weed's. People come to the beach in shorts and neon shirts and skimpy swimwear, not black, sagging and runkled old funeral suits. They swiftly bludgeoned Weed to the ground and dragged him and the woman and her kids away to the vans, provoking new intensities of terror and despair in the devastated refugee family.

Weed wailed to Bobette for help. She would tell the police who he was and what happened. However, Bobette was having problems of her own. She was bright yellow and shaking violently, wracked by some kind of violent seizure. Paramedics were stretchering her to an ambulance that was attending the melee. Bobette's mock gingham plastic ground sheet was trampled into the sand, the food and the hamper were scattered. A small egg sandwich impotently fluttered its top slice as it expired. Weed stretched out to it, to this last article of their first day out together, and had his fingers smacked with a truncheon.

Now, dumped in the back of a police van emblazoned with hamburger ads, and on the feet of the refugees already in there, Weed lost consciousness — not because of the blows he had received, but because he couldn't see the point in hanging on to it, not under these circumstances.

'You want to watch it, lad, hanging around in places like this,' said Inspector Yard to Weed in his seaside police cell. 'Saltwater is fatal to weeds. Or are you seaweed?'

The good inspector tootled.

'I heard they had someone from my manor in here, I had to pop up and gloat — I mean liaise with my colleagues.

'Anyway, your claim to have inadvertently pole axed that poor innocent illegal with a small item of artificial cheese has been corroborated. Though the story is very obviously a big festering pile of porky pies. Your collaborator —' he consulted one of the fleshy folds of his paw which presumably contained a notebook '— one Ms. Blobette Dope, was checked into St. Vitus' Mortuary —' Weed's eyes saucered in alarm. 'I mean Infirmary — suffering a violent metaphysical reaction to yellow paint.

'I'm not sure that's what they mean by giving her one, Weed, but whatever it takes to get them horizontal — or in your case, incapacitated — eh?

'Anyway, she talks the same rubbish as you, and as for your victim, we've nobody here that understands alien to fathom the rubbish she's talking, so it is with deep egret that I have to let you leaf. Ha ha ha! Weed — leaf? Nah? Never mind. You watch, you'll be telling it to your mates next week. They all crack in the end.

'By the way, it seems that it slipped your mind that you were working for Daikon AirCon — *are* working for Daikon AirCon. For the time being, at any rate. When it says in your contract to give a hand, it means to the cops, not the villains. Mind, with you on their side, I'm surprised the refugees weren't bouncing things off your head before the lads were. Well, we had to inform your erstwhile — I mean worthwhile — employers. They do like their rules.

'By the way, Weed — you don't mind if I call you Weed, or shall I call you hopeless bloody git? Did you know that daikon in Japanese means giant radish? And they are giant, Weed, the Japanese radishes. The shape of carrots and the dimensions of my wotsit, my sense of humour. And you don't want to get shafted by something that size, do you?'

With all the grace and alacrity of a bubble in a lava lamp, Yard wobbled himself into an extravagant disco pose with an emasculated 'Ow!' that sent all the neighbourhood dogs into frenzy and hysteria, and caused permanent hearing impairment to all the bats in his belfry. Then, burbling like a toddler who has just found the cat flap in the back of the sweet shop, he squeezed out the cell door and did that famous forward-backward moon walk down the hallway, singing something which might have been a terribly famous pop song, but which was definitely bad.

That was how Weed met Inspector Yard for the first time.

None of this remembering is helping Weed find Bobette. On the pavement outside Perseverance House he reasserted his own sense of his own worth and capability. He resolved to find Bobette himself.

The first job was to find a cafe for a lucky pot of tea and half a packet of fidgety cigarettes. He continued by standing outside the Daikon AirCon HQ hopping from one foot to another, wondering where he might find a public lavatory.

Eventually, he thought he might try his flat in case he'd given Bobette his address after all. By this time it was so late the trains had stopped and he had to walk too many kilometres through the poisonous dark of the city to get home. Bobette wasn't there.

He decided to check the other Daikon AirCon buildings in the city. It was now dawn and a few cafes were opening up which afforded Weed a few more lucky pots of tea. He spent all Saturday patrolling Daikon AirCon network in the city without luck. Overwrought and without food or sleep, Weed eventually passed out slumped over his teapot in yet another cafe.

When he came to, he was being licked all over by large and earnest Alsatian dogs. He was lying on his back on the cold concrete floor of a police dog pen.

Called to police the passed out Weed in the cafe, the cops could find no evidence of conventional intoxication. No smell of booze, no Windolene around the mouth, and no diced carrots in the pockets. They decided he was on The Hard Stuff and had taken him down the nick for the sniffer dogs to have a go at.

All the tea in his system was making the normally hormonal hounds feel quite peaceful and mellow.

Behind the dreamy, happy pooches, blocking out the light and most of the known universe was the congenitally grinning Inspector Yard.

They're licking you like they found their long lost mummy,' he drooled. 'And I know that ain't so 'cos I grew 'em in test tubes myself.

'What have you been doing, you naughty little boy? I think you'd better stay here till we find out.'

When the blood tests came back from forensics it was Tuesday. It was nearly four days since he had set off to find Bobette and three since being admitted unconscious to the dog pen. He had missed his weekend sales excursion to the countryside and two days of work and training. Much worse he was hopelessly detached from the woman he was otherwise destined to marry, make babies and live happily ever after with. The blood tests showed Weed to be 100 percent free of drugs but 50 percent Darjeeling. A portable Alpha Squad was wheeled in.

A scan showed instantly that, apart from caffeine and tannin, Weed was full of severe emotional distress and suffering concomitant intellectual impairment and that his apparent narcolepsy was actually a form of catatonia induced by trauma, exhaustion, and disillusion.

'The kid couldn't be more messed up if he was a cake shop full of monkeys,' announced Yard expertly.

So they let him go, tipped him out on the street — bearded, a scarecrow, best and only suit covered in doggy drool — straight into the arms of a rapidly perambulating Ms. Wap.

'Ah! Robert!' she sparkled. 'We've missed you. I've set up a meeting with Mr. Stonewall for tomorrow, you'll be glad to know.

'Now are you going to get yourself cleaned up? You're very lucky because the Core 171 workshop, "The Great Ascent: stairs vs. elevators", is beginning in just 35 minutes in Sam Smiles House. You'll have to get your skates on if you're going to visit the barber and a dry cleaner — what is that? Rottweiler or Alsatian?

'Don't worry, Robert. We'll see Mr. Stonewall tomorrow and I'm sure everything will be all right.

'I imagine you've done plenty of prep — I hear one has plenty of time in prison.'

'We are all very disappointed in you Bob,' said Ms. Wap. 'Very disappointed.'

Weed was very disappointed too and in more ways than either Ms. Wap or Slater Stonewall could possibly imagine.

Slater Stonewall, HND, MF, floated past, simultaneously looking very disappointed and tapping at a laptop. He said nothing. This was Ms. Wap's show — she was proving herself excellent junior management, laying it down for Weed like this and remaining unflapped by the zero-G, while Weed flapped his arms and legs like an inebriated heron. He was also quiet because he was savouring the feeling of being in control, in his element, on his manor; he was savouring the sensation of success: band three manager, wife, two kids, one large car, one small one, a four-bedroom house in a leafy suburb, and at the age of only thirty-five he still had plenty of time to make band five or even six and buy a pony for his daughter. He was also quiet merely because he enjoyed the amniotic quality of zero-G, the maternal hum of Ms. Wap's voice and the odd opportunity to get a glimpse up her skirt as they floated by each other.

'We had faith in you Bob. You are a bright lad, you have qualifications — your father evidently made a lot of sacrifices on your behalf, Bob, not only sending you to school but also on to university afterwards.'

Weed had finished school and gone on to university to study physics because his cousin had won a bunch of education coupons on the lottery — one of those gimmick prizes designed to make gambling look more like improving yourself and less like gambling. The cousin didn't want them because he had his heart set on being a police officer and had dumped the coupons on Weed in exchange for a deceased hamster. Into the bargain, he got rid of Weed who he thought of as a sap and an embarrassment to the family. The cousin wanted him banged up in the cloisters of academia, and not dragging his acne round the estate where all and sundry could see him.

Weed had done well on his course but the coupons didn't stretch to an MA which was the only route to a meaningful job where he used what he had learned, and there wasn't any other money coming from anywhere to keep him at college. Now the ordinary demands of life and a multinational electronics corporation were ruling out even studying part time which was a shame because Weed was, actually despite his shambolic appearance and nonevent of a life, an undiscovered scientific genius. Well, look at it from Daikon AirCon's point of view. They liked to keep their workers happily busy in facile displays of commitment because the smile training programme was expensive to develop and the company didn't want its employees skipping off to decent jobs.

'I wonder how your father's going to feel about this conversation when he hears about it. Is he going to be pleased do you think Bob?'

Weed was enjoying zero-G. He was pretending to be a fish. Being a fish was a bit like being a bird with all its soaring, swooping and freedom, but being a fish was more fun than being a bird because the ocean is a mysterious place, full of light and colour and also unimaginable blackness; warm and light and cold and heavy; and at every turn there was some new and unlikely creature or weed or coral. Nature must have had a great time creating the ocean: and it is clear evidence that nature has a sense of humour.

Weed was also being a fish because he didn't particularly care what Ms. Wap or Mr. Stonewall thought of him any more. They, on behalf of Daikon AirCon had made up their minds that he was untrustworthy, unreliable, slippery, dishonest, rebellious, stubborn, subversive, stupid, possibly unbalanced, perhaps dangerous and definitely congenitally useless — while Weed had decided that he was a fish. It all seemed very equitable and definitively settled.

'We gave you this job in good faith, Bob,' Ms. Wap was continuing. 'You assured us repeatedly you wanted to be a good salesmanperson, that you had drive and ambition and guts and were a motivated self-starter. Yet from the day you started you have consistently demonstrated that you have a poor attitude. Where does this bad attitude come from, Bob? Did we do something wrong? We have tried to nurture you, Bob, to give you every chance to develop into a first class salesmanperson and we have extended a helping hand and given you a leg up. We have been a sympathetic ear and a shoulder for you to cry on. Yet it remains that in eight months of intensive training and innumerable opportunities in the field, you have failed to sell a single air conditioner, except those few days you were clearly not yourself.

'Is this perversity on your part, Bob? Or something else? It's not that you are belligerent. You just seem to lack ... spirit ... bones ... life ... And lacking spirit is about the same as lacking soul, Bob. Do you know what soul is, Bob? Have you ever thought about soul? It's the animating principle, Bob. Without soul we are just machines — or something hanging in an abattoir. You might go as far as to say that the soul is like a ghost because it's the thing that comes out of the body when we die. And if the body is sometimes like a machine, then the soul is the ghost in the machine.

'Oh! Did you hear what I said? I just said the soul was like the ghost in the machine! I just thought of that, Bob. That's what happens when you make an effort and use your brain, you come up with original ideas and nice ways of putting them. And I owe it all to Daikon AirCon because they are the ones who challenge me to be all I can be, and inspire me to think day after day after day.

'So, soul is the divine spark given us by a non-specific, pluralistic kind of god because we have customers on every continent, Bob. Imagine that! Customers absolutely all over the world ... And we have been given this soul — and we should be grateful for it because it was given to us and we didn't have to pay for it — so we can exercise it and make the most of it and maximise our abilities through it and thereby make the best of ourselves —'

Stonewall was not enormously comfortable with this soul stuff, even though it was sanctioned at the highest level: wasn't Daikon AirCon supposed to stay out of politics?

'Bob? Do you believe yourself to be a whole person? You don't behave like one.'

Weed at the moment believed himself to be a whole fish and said nothing — fish are not famous for their loquacity.

So Stonewall spoke instead. 'Now go away and reflect on what we have said, Bob. Reflect long and reflect deeply. Reflect all the way into the core of your being, and then resurface baptised in the fast strong currents of your soul, come up radiant and cleansed and rebuilt like a born-again salesmanperson For there is no space at Daikon's inn for the tentative at heart. You're fired.'

And so ended Weed's short career as a sales rep. And then he went down the pub and drank like the fish he had been pretending to be.

The jobless Weed signed on, which was easy. Eventually.

The benefit officers were in a bit of a flap the first day Weed went in. A quarter of their number had just been axed, downsized, streamlined, and outsourced. They stared irritably at incomplete and broken data on their seats, at files that hadn't been updated because the person tasked with that updating was now sitting on the other side of the desk in the very long queue with Weed.

Eventually they got to Weed, told him to go away and come back again another day. When he had done that, they told him to go away and fill out some forms online, which he could have done without coming into the office. He did that and when he came in for his next appointement, they told him to go away and fill out some more forms online, which demanded the same information he had given the first forms. When he had done that and came in again as per instructions, he was simply told to go away.

Eventually they called him in to sign his Contract of Unemployment, and when he had signed, they told him that although contractually unemployed and therefore legally bound to find a job within 21 working days or be liable to a fine, sanction or imprisonment, they were not going to actually pay him unemployment benefit because Daikon AirCon claimed he hadn't really tried and therefore, ipso facto, was culpable for his current unemployment. He should therefore travel across town to another department where he should wait in another very long line because they too would need to refuse him any help. He could make a futile appeal which would make him subject to random searches of his body and home by Benefit Investigators, the Police, and anybody else who wanted to. As a valued customer he should have a nice day and next please.

'But I have a mortgage — how am I going to ...'

'You were no doubt apprised of the risks, liabilities and responsibilities of such commitments. The department has no provisions for supporting the impetuous. You shouldn't have squandered your job. Next!'

'Damage limitation, innit' said Warren bravely. 'Have to sell the cow.'

He put a steadying hand on Weed's shoulder, which was both brotherly and useful, because Weed's shoulder was at 45 degrees to the floor and about to hit it.

Weed spluttered and whimpered simultaneously. He was not being as brave as Warren: it was not Warren's stuff that was being sold, it was his own. All of his own stuff.

The rotisserie had gone first. That had been very easy because Weed hadn't known, and still didn't know, what a rotisserie was. He never seemed to have the time to unpack it and find out, and he never had the heart to ask his father who had insisted he needed one and was very enthusiastic about it. He got quite a good price for it, almost enough to pay off half the HP on it. Then he sold the tv and his Mexican rug. And then he sold the cooker.

And now he was to sell the books. And more importantly, the cow.

When he had made this decision the previous day, the tachyon drive machine that at once would take people back in time and make his future, disappeared. It was gone; inextricably lodged in some remote plane of possibility. The only remaining part was the chassis which was the only bit Weed had finished in current time and which for a while was in the living room doubling as a coffee table until the coffee had run out.

Now his income has gone and he packs his aspirations into a used toilet paper carton and readies himself to take them down to Spunky's Porno Emporium.

'What else is there?' asked Warren. 'You could try selling the mould. I know a few kids would buy it just in case it was psychedelic. You could try the walls at that used paint shop.'

Weed's other possessions after paying his mortgage this month and the interest on the rotisserie amounted to: a huge pile of kebab wrappers, a sink full of used tea bags and an old coffee tin overflowing with cigarette butts.

Warren offered Weed a rusty nail. 'Don't have a bullet for you to bite on. Chew on this.'

Downstairs, Weed lashed the box of books to the back of the cow and then unlashed Ermintrude from a pylon of the bike shed. Warren made a sniffy excuse about his hymen growing back and how if he didn't get horizontal with a girl — preferably Sharon in procurements, though it was not likely she would be in his local, the Bucket of Vomit — he was going to get horizontal with lager, and he made off for the pub.

Odd. Warren's sniffiness wasn't entirely the kind that would come from the line of amphetamines that he had hoovered up just before going out.

Weed numbly navigated the cow through the poo and the glass, toward the High Street and down to the porn shop. There was nowhere else that would take books or magazines or cows. Especially not the pawnshop, which was getting quite exclusive, snooty even, and was accepting only things it thought it had a rat's chance of selling again, such as gold teeth, guns or heroine.

The old guy who ran the porn shop was totally blind and carried an extensive collection of used porn bought from the local community. Or so he thought. Because of his disability he was obliged to ask the prospective supplier to describe the pictures to him when deciding whether to buy. If you could concoct a reasonable description of little girls and donkeys, hose pipes and buckets, he would take anything that felt papery. Consequently his shop was a dusty trove of old school textbooks, telephone directories and home shopping catalogues. His business was kept alive by the constant stream of social anthropologists, antiquarians, palaeontologists and all kinds of ad designers and copywriters. The academics found the porn shop to be a unique deposit of social and cultural artefacts that provided at one source a complete description of the minutiae of everyday life, a fossilised footprint of working class mores, dreams and aspirations that in and of itself constituted a complex codified social discourse. The ad people just liked to get heated over the children's underwear pages in the home shopping catalogues.

It was Weed's plan to tell Spunky that his astronautics books were some pretty hot donkey and little girl items and that Ermintrude was the actual donkey from the photos.

Warren had wondered 'What if Spunky notices she's not a male donkey hung like an elephant, that she's a female cow, complete in every anatomical respect? I mean, the udders should keep him confused for a while, but what when ...?' Weed was staring at him. Warren stopped. They both knew what would happen when Spunky twigged. It had been a silly question.

'Better than hamburgers from Ermintrude's point of view.' Weed observed hopefully.

'Gives you a twinge, though.'

'Not the kind of twinge Spunky will give her.'

Weed led the docile cow away for the last time and immediately teams of shaven-headed, jackbooted thugs descended on the big pile of dung she had left behind and began shovelling it into shopping bags. Unless Spunky was seriously developing his scat collection, they were planning to sell it as fertiliser at the allotments.

The cow lurched violently to the right and into the metal grille on the front of the betting shop. The betting shop was the focus of all sorts of activity some of which had lots to do with gambling of one sport or another, some of which had to do with gambling with your life and well being. One of the most popular bets was, being within the boundaries of the estate, on the bookies' still being there in the morning.

Ermintrude had smelled the discarded packaging and syringes of elicit and potent substances tossed there by the estate's chemical fraternity. Of particular interest in the rubbish was the wraps of steroids and antibiotics. This was included among the usual heroin and speed by those many who took anything in the hope of achieving a synergistic reaction with the other powders and pills they took and just because it was bad for them. The steroids and the antibiotics evidently reminded Ermintrude of the factory farm she had been born on, and evoked powerful calfhood memories of the farmer coming round and injecting them with the stuff everyday. The cow was not going to move from this spot. The cow had come home, it had found the mummy it had been prematurely wrenched from — the cow was a junky and was busting for a fix. Numb and indifferent though he was, Weed tugged at the animal, urging it along and out of the estate before they were both scavenged. When all else had gone pear shaped he wanted just one thing to work out right.

When the tugging had no effect, Weed grabbed her head in a big, tight arm lock and began to pry the beast away from the pharmaceuticals.

'Got some lifting gear. Sort you out no time.'

'Great,' Weed might have thought had he not been numb and indifferent, 'Let's get the cow on the back of your lorry and you'll be off with it down the supermarket before I've got my finger out of my nose.' Weed assumed someone was trying to steal his cow.

'Lifting gear? Did I say lifting gear?' The speaker chuckled and shook his head at the folly of pronouncing "exotic vegetable clippings" as "lifting gear".

'Lord know I meant wicked gear. But I see you numb and indifferent. Well, this gear make you different, that for sure.'

Weed looked up from his cow wrestling to see an old man leaning on the doorframe of the shop chewing rather than puffing on a comfortable looking old pipe. His mischievous face seemed to be made of shiny vinyl that had been shoved roughly between his hat and his collar. He looked like a happy plastic bag.

'Just thought I'd mention it.'

Weed was now trying to tilt the cow on its side.

'You in some kind of jam there?'

Weed was now sidling limbo fashion beneath Ermintrude.

'Sort you out right away. After you had your milk.' Then as if Weed had just declined a selfless offer of help, 'Well, it's your thing.'

Meanwhile, Weed, who was crablike under the animal, was heaving like a trainee Atlas. Ermintrude continued munching optimistically on the junky wraps, quite unmoved by Weed's huffings and puffings.

At the age of 24 Weed had botched his life. Now he was making a mess of his own dissolution.

'Used to be a reading man myself. I suppose you used to be a reading man too. Used to be, because if you still were you wouldn't be doing what you doing now.

'Maybe the books don't want to go. Maybe they be clinging on for dear life. Maybe they don't want to be separated from you. Maybe the cow don't want to go. Maybe the cow got a hot tip about the 3:40. Maybe she heard it from the horse's mouth.'

Weed was still under Ermintrude, face down, on all fours, straining to raise the beast on his back.

'You seem pretty determined to get rid of them,' observed the old bloke whose pipe was making some interesting odours. 'You in a state of desperation? Up the dire straights without a paddle?

'Sort you out right away.

'Like I say, used to read quite a lot. Shakespeare, Kant, Aristotle, Plato, Sartre, Descartes, Goethe, Aquinas. Voltaire. Dostoevsky. Thought it would make me a wiser and better person.

'Balzac!

'Thought maybe one of these books would say something that would make everything suddenly make sense. Eventually it occurred to me that if this was so they would put it in the blurb on the back. You know. "Angela Smartpants had everything. Looks, money, boyfriend, a fantastic creative job. Until one day, in a chance encounter, an incredibly important computer disc that will make her company even richer is stolen. Recovering the information, immerses her in international intrigue and has her hobnobbing with the rich and famous. The story contains graphic sex and the meaning of life."'

Weed had managed to wrap himself round the cow like a human spanner and was attempting to wrench it away from the shop front.

'I tell you, what them books need is a good home. Spunky's Porno Emporium is not the best environment for a sensitive, intelligent book. Or cow. I tell you what. Sacred though the cow may be, I take her off your hands for fair exchange that will sort you out in no time, and you — we all — be on our way. Fancy taking a look at a book again now I have time on my hands. Maybe it be a waste of time. Less hectic gamble than in there anyway,' jabbing his pipe at the bookie's. 'Anyway, I fed up with paying those jackbooted thugs for my fertiliser at the allotments. I don't even have an allotment. But enough of my trade secrets. Maybe the cow frighten off the jack boots. Maybe if I dock the tail they think it some kind of enormous Rottweiler. Only cow they ever met was under ketchup.'

Weed had both feet braced against the metal work and was pulling with all his might on Ermintrude's ears, so the old fellow merely dangled the clear plastic bag above Weed's nose.

Weed could smell the draw through the plastic. His nose wiggled visibly and followed the bag as it wobbled in the small breeze.

'This for the books and the cow. I give them a good home. They come with me no trouble. Old friends, you see. You go get off your face.

'A mutually advantageous proposition.'

Weed looked into the bag and saw oblivion. He didn't assess the nutritional worth of smoked heads against the nutrition his books would buy. He calculated not the street value of this huge bag of herb against the resale value of the hundred weight of pristine astronautics texts and a slightly used cow. He just saw a black hole for all the rubbish in his head: the thick nebulae of poisoned emotions, the red dwarves of his ambitions, the cold moons of desire, the stray comets of reason, and the frozen gases of failure.

'It's magic,' advised the old man.

Weed let go of Ermintrude's head and seized the bag. If the anal retentive we all carry in our head had said anything about exchanging the last of his wealth for a sack of dried leaves and twigs and seeds, he didn't hear it.

You'll be needing this,' added the old man, handing him a large box of corn flakes.

' 'Ello, 'ello, 'ello.'

'Learning French, Inspector Yard?' asked the old man without turning round to see who had just crept up behind him.

'Corrupting innocents?' asked Inspector Yard.

'Oh, my innocence is incorruptible, you know that Inspector Yard,' chuckled the old man. He didn't need to look round; he knew who he was talking to.

'I was worried about the cow. You're as innocent as Doctor Evil, you are,' said Yard. Then clocking Weed, 'Walpurgis Night? Or has the Scrubs become an open prison? You got a license for them books? Dangerous things books. Can make your head go all funny and start you thinking weird.'

'Just a little bibliographical exchange. I sorting the lad out.'

'Little? Well, if I hear a library's been mugged, I'll know where to come looking.

'Anyway, what do you want with books? You can't smoke them. You can't shoot them. Have you discovered some hallucinogen in the ink? Astronautics?' Yard enquired, looking at the titles of the books. 'Astronautics is not your kind of getting spaced. Hate to be the one to tell you.'

Yard circled Weed as best a big roly-poly blob can circle anything.

'A mind's a terrible thing to waste. Your adventures in narcosis have already cost you your job. Band 27 salesman. Bottom rung of a very long ladder. But you're a lad with able knees. A thinking job, selling things. Takes brains to sell things. Takes brains to remember all that patter Daikon scripts for you. And there's real genius in writing it too. Genius to write all that bullshit and believe in it. Amazing. But where there's shit there's brass.

'Supremely important job, sales: makes the world go round, that clinking, clunking, squelching sound.'

Weed, whose brains had been turned to a peculiarly rigid mush by his job, heard nothing. With his hand inserted in the front of his underpants clutching his bag, he waited for Yard to wobble or roll or blob away.

'Me, my job's to pick up those that have stopped thinking right. The dysfunctional bits and Bobs. Like a gardener: pulling up all the Weeds you don't want growing in your garden. A lowly Parks and Benches Operative. Not the same kind of thinking.

'The brain's a terrible thing to waste, Weed.

'By the way,' now addressing the old man, 'There's a well weird Weed on the streets these days — and if I find you been selling him stuff to make him weird, I'll take you somewhere where you'll have to listen to my jokes for a very long time.'

And Yard was gone, vanishing into the daylight as abruptly as he had emerged from it, leaving only a dimension-popping guffaw behind to rattle the windows and worry the rats.

'That wasn't even a little bit close,' said the old man.

'We all sorted then.' And with that, he took Ermintrude's leash and turned away.

With a simple grace that belied its ungulate nature, the cow abandoned the drug wrappers as if it had only been pretending to care. And with Ermintrude in tow, the old man was gone as abruptly and emphatically as Yard a second before.

Outside the estate were horns and crowds: a solid wall of movement on the High Street. Inside the estate, for once, was calm. And there seemed set out for him a clear and ready path through the crush and rubble, back to Nirvana Heights. The only way to go. So that's the way

Weed went back into the heart, the keep of his adult being, his citizenship; back to his soon-to-be-repossessed flat.

Weed settled down to the following course of action. First he would smoke as much as possible as quickly as possible. Then he would forget about everything and become a vegetable. Finally — probably before supper time tonight — he would be arrested when the Alpha Squads picked up his illegal state of mind on their scanners.

He would be in jail in time for breakfast on Tuesday morning at the latest. They always served tea with flaccid, spongy bread and spready things that seemed to sap health from your body. He didn't look forward to prison, he didn't *not* look forward to prison. He didn't care.

So home, Robert, and don't spare the skins!

Keeping the corn flakes close to hand, he sat down to his first smoke. His muscles melted and became warm buttery pods between his bones. Peace, like the dark of a spring night, seeped in and flooded his brainpan and trickled down inside his neck to fill up the rest of him. And it occurred to him that this was the first time he had relaxed in as long as he could remember.

It was indeed magic weed.

He lay down and wondered where Bobette was and waited for the police.

Weed is no more. Weed is expunged. Weed is deleted. He has ceased to think and is waiting to be pulled up by his roots and tossed in Yard's bin.

There is nothing left to do.

Yard pushes, squeezes and barges his way through the jungle interior of Nirvana Heights. He is alone, he has become separated from the Executive Action Group — or they have become separated from him.

After his battle with the dead Mr. Perkins and after the Executive Action Group arrived too late to save him from the killer salad — not that he needed any help, anyway — he had set off with the group to sort out this dread menace that threatened to turn the world green. But this darn vegetable wasn't going down without a fight.

Pugh at the rear of the thin blue line beating its way to the dark heart of tenement incognita was the first to go. He just disappeared. Not a sound, not a rustle or a holler — nothing. One minute he was there, the next he was very and completely gone.

Pew was next. He slipped from the path into the rubble-lipped maw of an unplanned atrium within the building.

For some wild-eyed seconds he hung or clung in the vines while his colleagues tried to reach him or made careful notes in their little black books. Then, as if pulled from below, he slipped ungracefully out of sight, his gristly knuckles stripping the skin from the creepers.

Pew had gone down. Barney McGrew went up. Some sudden whiplash of stem lifted him out of his boots and abruptly into the green hammocky loft of the building.

Tuffet, Dibble and Grout were removed by avalanche. A particularly dense knot which had been restraining an even bigger dense knot somewhere above them unravelled and poured free behind Yard and down the hall where the three laboured.

Yard's progress may have dislodged the vines. But Yard didn't think so.

Captain Flack was the last to go. He had been plagued by things in his eyes and leaves rubbing against him for most of the climb and after losing the last of his squad he went down with full-on hay fever. His eyes watered and swelled, and he sneezed to Yard that he just had to score some antihistamines and vanished.

So now Yard faces the dreadful thingy alone. Not that he's much bothered at the prospect. He has the measure of this outsized aspidistra now; he has it sussed and that's just about the same thing as having it bang to rights.

Think what we like about Inspector Yard, he is very intuitive. He has an uncanny sense for anything he disapproves of. He only has to take one look at a thing to be able to decide for or against it.

He is also very efficient. No sooner has he decided whether he approves of a thing than he sets about sorting it out. He'll often sort it out even if he approves of it as a precautionary measure against it slipping a later date into a state of which he might disapprove. When he disapproves of something he sorts it out until he either approves of it or at least feels pretty neutral about it. Once in a while he'll check back to find out whether the thing he had sorted out was also illegal. But that is definitely an optional part of the process. Disapproval was his guiding beacon, his lighthouse of morality. He couldn't much see the point of the legality issue because most of the law is merely a rationalisation of what one group of legislators or another approved or disapproved of or felt was good for them at one time or another, and Yard had long ago noticed that the sky tended not to fall in when jurisprudential opinion changed or when his own interpretation of the law made, say, black into white, or fish into ostriches, or bananas into offensive weapons.

Yard had decided that he very much didn't approve of this big green thingummy. In fact, he had disapproved of it as far back as before it had even existed. He had disapproved of it as far back as when that weird puff had hit the streets. And now, all alone and in full possession of the suss, he was going to sort out this weed, but good.

On he goes until the sense of building has been entirely lost and there are creepers and vines for wall, for ceiling and for floor. The place has taken on an odour that for a veggie would be exciting and spinachy, but which for our rotund and doughnutty policeman is unwholesome; something alien to be left on the plate, something to say 'yuck' at, something to be binned. Without visible aid to navigation and guided only by his sense of disapproval, he squeezes through the final curtain into a space from which the plant goes out rather than comes in a point from which the plant emanates rather than invades or strangles.

The orderly exiting of the plant allowed some of the walls to remain standing, though they were much denuded and estranged from each other and the ceiling. Evidently, this had been the pad of a young person with a weird perspective on the world. Pictures of stars, nebulae and galaxies, Einstein and Van Gogh were still tacked to the jagged teeth of plasterboard. Instead of three flying ducks, three flying space shuttles climbed the wall.

And in the middle of the room: the thing itself, the node of Yard's disapproval, the bulb of his ire.

The rhizome nestles on a mattress like a large yellow, greasy, translucent garlic. Green tubes fountain from its head and radiate from its base.

Yard approaches and shakes his head at the awe-inspiring temerity of the thingy's affront to his approval before unhinging his blade. He measures the flick-knife against the task before it with a few gentle hacking and carving motions in the air. It's quite obvious that this little blade would be just the thing when up against skinny young wide boys in their dancing shoes, but against a huge ugly rhizome he needs something a little less ... elegant, something a little more against regulations. Funnily enough he has just the thing lurking up his other sleeve: an eighteen inch machete, stowed there many years ago against just such an eventuality.

This blade tests with a gratifying whooshing in the air and he raises it above his head, or up to his ear, which is as far as his arm has ever reached — which accounts for the uncombed plume of knots rising on the top of his head above the well-groomed back and sides.

There was something of a foetal curl in the shape of the thingy like something human — perhaps a man — all balled up and doing nothing but sleeping and growing. Yard may or may not be taking this in as he surveys for the track of his first strike.

'One man went to mow, went to mow a meadow, One man went to mow and slash and hack,' he sings.

Yard swings and feels the machete knocked out of his hand to thung point-down in the floor. He feels the whoosh of his assailant's second assault as he blobs and weebles presciently out of the way. The attacker's weapon hums and thrums at Yard as he rolls out of the way, round and round the tuber thingy. He recognises the attacker, of course. It is Warren Wosisname from downstairs. Works the same place as the perp. Might have guessed they was in cahoots. In fact he had assumed as much. Been seen taking tea together. Nuff said.

Shame though. Warren seemed like a normal lad from the outside: football, lager, too much testosterone, sliced white bread, and petty larceny.

Yard knew of Warren because Yard had done checks on everyone in the entire building after Weed was lifted comatose and weird out of the cafe. Yard had run checks on everyone in the building on countless occasions in the past and so had known all about both Weed and Warren well before they had come to his attention. He had run so many checks partly because there were a lot of strange things to disapprove of in the Heavenly Estate and partly because he would hate to have thought he hadn't checked everyone in the estate — or indeed in the city. He had run all those checks because that was the kind of great galloon he was.

Warren, green blotchy, and quite insane in the vegetable light, was wielding a stout length of scaffolding, which was evidently the weapon. He obviously had some karate or kung fu in him — or had simply taken far to much speed. He is making some great moves: vicious jabs when you expect fulsome swings, fulsome swings when you expect vicious jabs; fast footwork following or anticipating the tack of Yard's evasions, the odd under thrust to tangle the legs — and all the while swinging from left to right to drive Yard away from the heart of the roots.

'Ooh! Shall we lance?' Yard invited the smaller man.

Of course the policeman could just shoot Warren. He is well within his rights, being in dire and immediate disapproval and all that, but in truth he is enjoying the occasion and the sport. He is enjoying the sheer, abject futility of Warren chasing him around trying to hit him with a length of pipe.

Warren still bleary with booze but held up by speed, thought he had better say something to assert himself more fully on the situation, though he wasn't doing too badly with the scaffolding. He came up with 'Back, Yard,' and then remembering some movies he had once seen, 'Your number's up.'

'My number's J007,' Yard corrected him. ' "Up" is a preposition.'

Alas, time snaps at our heels. He cannot stay there bobbling and giggling all day when there's a giant to battle. He waits for a swing at his body and steps into it. Warren's metal bar disappears into the folds of Yard's being with a schloop.

Yard shimmies a little to allow his prehensile flab a better grab on the weapon.

Warren is unprepared for this but recovers and drives the bar round and throws his weight on it in an attempt for the ribs.

'You are awful, but I like you,' the policeman tells Warren.

Yard giggles and squirms. 'Last Tango in plaster of Paris! Do be a dear and fetch the butter,' and with a big two-handed yank on the bar Yard tosses Warren — all 85 kilos of him — directly up through the leafy roof and possibly as far as outer space.

'Hasta la vista, erm ... wossyername.'

He expelled Warren's iron bar from his blubber and made a show of picking his teeth with it as he contentedly waddled back to his machete.

'Now, where was I?

He has seen on tv how Japanese chefs like to carve little sculptures out of vegetables — out of turnips, giant radishes, carrots, that sort of thing. They sculpted fish mostly. Yard never understood why one might want a radish-flavoured fish when you could have a fish-flavoured fish. He has seen them carve little girls pretty as the real thing, cats, dolphins — once even an entire full-size dress which was then worn by a real live woman. A woman in a radish dress — imagine that! Whatever the point of it, he fancied a piece of it. He was not without his creative side and he didn't believe in suppressing it. He thought he would make himself a ... tank. Or a giant hamburger. A truncheon? How about a great big pit bull? He is settling on the latter when Warren bursts through the ceiling, bovvers first, right on to the crown of Yard's cogitating bonce. Yard flops onto his side like a big tired beach ball and Warren tumbles safely through the rolls of the policeman's flab to finish with a bottom-grinding bump on the floor.

'Rats!' he complains. 'You're getting a bit skinny there, Inspector. Try to put on a little weight. I could have knackered my coccyx.'

Warren isn't daft. His brain hasn't been totally addled by American tv imports: he knows that Yard won't stay cherubically unconscious for the rest of the story or until it's too late for him to do anything to stop the good guys, and then wake faintly groggy to be led meekly and contritely away by the emergency services. In reality, he will wake unreasonable and bearish through concussion and try to dismantle anything within arm's reach. And he will do so at the most inconvenient moment.

He must get rid of Yard or humanity will face the consequences.

First, he can usefully lose Yard's weapons so if he does wake up he won't be able to immediately spoil everyone's fun.

He reaches for the machete and freezes: his scalp is tingling in an eerie manner; an eerie manner that signals an unseen presence, which signals that something in Warren's immediate vicinity is profoundly and fundamentally not right, which signals that, eerily, he is about to have his hair burned off by a lighted blowtorch. Warren thinks it better to forget about the machete and put his hands up, where his knuckles are immediately singed by a second blowtorch hovering near his scalp.

A woman's voice says 'Sorry,' and a man's voice says, 'Good morning, Warren.'

The man is Slater Stonewall, HND, MF, GBH. He is holding a blowtorch aimed at Warren's head. The woman is Ms. Wap and she is doing the same.

They both smile sweetly at him.

'We're a little concerned, Warren,' says Stonewall.

'We're a little concerned you're going to be late for work, Warren,' says Ms. Wap.

Both Ms. Wap and Stonewall were dressed immaculately as usual despite the long and arduous climb through this towering forest. Blue pinstripe for Ms. Wap, a knee-length skirt and big shouldered jacket and almost the same for Stonewall — both seemed to be into some kind of corporate gangster chic.

'Yes, you're right,' says Warren 'I'm going to be late for work if I don't watch it. Best be off before you start wondering where I've got to, eh?'

Hands on head he backs toward his best guess for the location of the door. 'And if you don't mind me saying,' sneaking a look at his watch, 'don't you have to clock in and all? No offence.'

'Oh, we started early today, Warren.'

'We're already on the job.'

'Well on the job.'

'Early risers.'

'Self-starters.'

'Got to get ahead of the game.'

'The early bird catches the rhizome, eh,' suggests Warren.

'We attended Daikon AirCon's excellent seminar on getting ahead.'

'Get a hat, eh? Nice one!'

'You should have been there, Warren. Would have done wonders for your career.'

'A hat takes less time. Anyway, not open to non-executive staff,' Warren pointed out.

Rather than seeing him out of what was left of Weed's room, the two supervisors have cut him off from the door and are stalking after him forcing him to circle the room backwards, still with his hands on his head as if trying to undo what he had earlier done to Yard. They hold their blowtorches out before them like they are .38 Specials. The flames are hard blue eyes in the dark and restless forest, the eyes of wraiths or huge pointy-backed beasts with blue worsted fur.

'Not that you've done so badly today, Warren.'

'No indeed, you've shown the grit and tenacity and initiative we would expect of a salesman rather than a clerk!'

'Congratulations, Warren!'

'Well you do what you can. I mean in a corporate relationship give and take is, is ... central ... '

'Pivotal even.'

'In the middle, you could say,' Warren elaborated warming to this new-found common ground.

'Exactly, Warren. You give, we take. What could be more balanced than that?'

'A tightrope walker with his granny balanced on his chin? A one-legged hippo in a minefield?' he suggested.

'In fact when we've got our little project finished here today we might ask you to try the Sales Department's Exceptional Entry Test for Exemplary Minions.'

'Everybody, but everybody has a good outside chance of passing.'

'You might make something of yourself after all.'

'Ah well, cheers like. I'm that eager, we could all go and get started now. No sense in wasting a nice morning if that's what it is. What do you say? And we could get some breakfast on the way. I'm famished.'

'But you would need to attend an intensive re-educational, I'm afraid.'

'You have spent far too much time close to that thing,' said Stonewall nodding at the rhizome, and the acid in his pronunciation of 'thing' nearly burned a hole in his tie.

'Your perspective is way out of kilt,' Ms. Wap explained.

'I'm not wearing a kilt, but if my flies are undone you can tell me straight.'

Stonewall and Ms. Wap menace Warren's nose with a few deft and whooshing jabs.

'You trotted on to the level playing field wearing the wrong shirt today, Warren.'

'And we're still not sure you know which is the winning team.'

'Ah well, kiss of death my support. Last time I picked a team to support, it was relegated the same season, their ground caught fire, and the manager was arrested for being a dirty sock fetishist. I was trying to help you out as it happens. I figured if I appeared to defect to the salad, luck would fall your side and we could all go home and get on with things.

'Why are we having this conversation, by the way?'

'Hush, Warren.'

'You and that Weed could have spoiled everything for everyone.'

Warren stumbles on roots as the flames leap ever closer. He can feel their hot doggy tongues wiping the sweat from his cheeks and ears as the two middle managers bound and spring and run at him, and he stumbles and flails in full reverse.

'You nearly ruined it all,' Ms. Wap told Warren.

'Thank goodness we had our eyes on the ball,' said Stonewall with evident satisfaction at a job well done.

'Do you know what his thing is about?'

'Do you know what it means, Warren?'

'This is God's punishment for me not eating my greens when I was a kid? We'll all be eating spinach fritters till next Christmas? Meat and two veg will become meat and 137 veg?'

Stonewall paused to gesticulate unnecessarily at the foliage around them. 'This huge ... triffid, this insane mutant daisy is going to take over the city.'

'It's going to take over Daikon AirCon,' continued Ms. Wap for him.

'It's going to take us over ...'

'Ditto everything, Warren.'

'Everything will stop, Warren.'

'Talking of stopping — I don't know if it's the decor or all this gyrating, but I think I'm going to throw.'

A swiping blowtorch scorches Warren's nose. His feet snare in the viney tangle on the floor and he goes sprawling. Lying on his back he is defenceless against Wap and Stonewall whose flames flick and whoosh over him like huge demented fireflies — OK, fireflies aren't dangerous. Perhaps the flames flick and whoosh like small, demented dragons. Stonewall stands astride Warren like a big game hunter squaring up for the coup de grace — or, given that big game hunters are not known for consorting with small demented dragons, perhaps he is more like a dragon-handling warlock squaring up for the coup de grace like a big game hunter.

However, Stonewall stops, stays his blow, putting an abrupt end to the turgid flow of similes in Warren's busy head.

He falls into digression: he has a need to explain something to Warren before he irrevocably singes his hair and boils his eyes in their sockets. Now Warren knows he has won the day. Long expositions by insane villains to beleaguered heroes are always the villain's downfall. The good guy's head is locked in the spiny vice of the huge henchman's steel jaws while a tarantula crawls across his nose. One unauthorised move means crunchy and splattery death. But now the villain pauses, squishes the tarantula and tells the good guy at length how once the toxic spores are unwittingly released into the atmosphere from the diva's compact in the presence of every national leader in the world assembled at the opera hall to attend a concert celebrating world peace and unity, killing them and millions of innocents dead, he, Max Mandrill, taking advantage of the ensuing lawlessness and confusion will call snap elections in all the leaderless nations, intercept all the ballot papers, personally fill in his name on every one, thereby creating the impenetrable illusion that all the eligible voters on the planet had spontaneously voted for him. But first, he Max Mandrill, is going to dunk our hero in a vat full of sulphuric acid and acid resistant piranhas. While the villain is explaining all this, our hero has got his puff back and has recalled the module in basic training titled *Day 76, Core 3, Escaping death in a pool full of acid and acid-resistant piranhas: in the nick of time — evasion, countermeasures and drying without a towel.* Having escaped, our hero makes it to the opera, slips into a tux and hoovers the spores directly into his own nasal membranes through a rolled bank note providentially provided by the clever chaps in the high-tech tricks department, where they will be safely neutralised by the antitoxin which he still has to recover from the huge henchman, although this will involve trekking through a snake infested jungle to the tomb of the vengeful Mayan demigod Ah Drat with the pathogens already eating his box office takings from the inside out.

The truly on-the-ball arch enemy should learn to do away with the spiders, the acid, the cannibal giants, the fish, the Mayan demi-gods, and go for the bullet in the back of the head at the earliest opportunity: bang, splat. No explanation, no bother, no problem, no hero.

Stonewall, is rolling bits of air between thumb and forefinger.

'Look at this stuff! Look at it! Cleaned, filtered; oxygen, carbon, nitrogen, water ... water content a bit high, — but,' he sniffs the bit of air he is rolling between his fingers, — 'so is the oxygen content. Quite stimulating even.'

'Triffic,' asserted Warren, surreptitiously working his way into a crouch, twisting his legs beneath him, and wriggling in the vegetable mess. 'That's us sorted then, innit. Daikon's mission to provide clean air to all the world is complete.'

'But that's just it!' exclaimed Ms. Wap.

'We didn't do it,' Stonewall went on.

'It was done, Warren.'

'Or rather, it just happened.'

'There was no executive decision.'

'No business proposal ...'

'No business plan ...'

'No outside consultation ...'

'No studies to ensure that it had an impact on the environment ...'

'Looks like an environment to me,' said Warren reasonably.

'There were no pally, chummy meetings with digestive biscuits and machined coffee.'

'And we haven't put our stamp, our mark on any of this.'

'This plant' said Stonewall, calmly mad, and waving one of the plant's tentacular trunks, 'is a giant bloody air conditioner.'

'Like I said, from triffid to triffic. Tell you what, though. You can sell it as the self-delivering, self installing air conditioner. It'll be all over the client's gaff before they get home. And think of the savings in overheads which can be passed on to the valued customer making Daikon AirCon ever more competitive. It's an idea that could catch on. In fact I think it is catching on whether we want it or not.'

'Oh dear.'

'Poor Warren.'

'You'll have to do better than that.'

'You just don't get it, do you.'

'That place on the Exceptional Entry Test is slipping away from you.'

'You see, Warren, we can't have this thing cleaning up the atmosphere on its own.'

'It isn't trained, Warren.'

'We'd love to just let it do its own thing ... but it just isn't trained.'

'And if it isn't trained, well we just don't know what it's going to do, do we.'

'Or when it's going to do it.'

'Or whether it'll do it properly, by the book.'

'And that could lead to all sorts of consistency issues.'

'And efficiency studies.'

'But ...' ventured Warren, indicating the rhizome.

'Wrong kind of training, Warren,' says Ms. Wap very sweetly.

'Sales, you see.'

'This is an environmental solutions issue.'

'He doesn't have the data.'

'Or the overalls.'

'Or the right kind of employee number.'

'It's an entirely different pay band.'

'Silly me,' acknowledged Warren. 'Never seen a green Environmental Engineering Processes and Solutions Engineer, now you come to mention it. Not one this size, anyways.'

'In that case, let's get to work, shall we?' Stonewall spirits his bonsai clippers from his pocket, clacking them testingly a few times.'

'Right, indeed,' concurs Warren as he springs tigerishly at Stonewall only to disappear through a hidden hole in the floor.

'Oh dear, Warren. And you really did come so close to getting a place on our course.'

'Nothing like a spot of competition to sort out the high fliers from the plummeters,' announces Stonewall with lip-smacking satisfaction and the clippers go on clacking as if sharing his happiness.

'The art of bonsai,' said Ms. Wap to Mr. Stonewall. 'Clip the young juicy growths first. Conserve trained and tested maturity only within the parameters of the form and encourage new growth only when absolutely necessary. New growth can be inducted in the following circumstances: death or careless pruning. You taught me that.' Said Ms. Wap in a corporately adoring sort of tone as if Stonewall were a horribly efficient new system for processing employees' time sheets.

'No maturity evident here,' announces Stonewall confidently as he tests his clippers on a few fronds.

'I think I'll sing my favourite ditty to enhance the enjoyment of the task.

If my heart were a tree,
It would be free,
And if my heart were free
It would cost no mone-ey,
And my salary-y
Would be nothing at all,
So I'm very happy-y
My heart's not a tree after all.'

The rhizome, bulb, or thingy is about shoulder height to a tall person or would tower over an unusually short one. At head height to the tall person or out of sight above the bulging waist to the short person, a spray of thick green trunks arcs into the vegetable dark. It is here that

Stonewall is going to start. He intends to separate the bulb from the foliage and the roots.

Ms. Wap reaches into the pack of giant leeky things, tugs one free and down for Stonewall to get a clear snip. Together they recoil as the most hideous thing they have ever seen is thereby exposed. Perched atop the thingy, pinched between the stalks and looking like a giant blob of greenish, greyish sausage meat, is the head of Inspector Yard. Its tongue dangles and drips and its eyes are rolled at zombie angles into the top of its head.

'Fee-fi-fo-fum, I smell the blood of a lazy bum,' it gurgles. 'Poor Weed. Always was a bit of a sap.'

The head opened wide and screeched and gurgled and howled and gibbered, frothed and sprayed spit and drool as it was sucked and dragged into the fibrous intestines of this most dreadful thingy, there surely to be digested, separated into his component molecules and redistributed through the plant's many parts.

The leaves and stems and branches of the thing waved and thrashed in the ecstasy of the moment, while Stonewall checked his watch, adjusted his immaculately aligned collar and cuff, and pointed out a withered shred of leaf in Ms. Wap's bolted-down hairdo. Eventually, he fired off a cheerful greeting when a not-digested-after-all Yard hove into view round the rhizome melodramatically shaking the branches and making what he felt to be black lagoon creature sound effects, which he punctuated with chuckles and fnarrs.

'Hadjergoin! You thought the thingy'd had me, dincha!'

Normally a match in size and pallor for the rhizome, the Inspector was much stained by his adventures. He looked like gargantuan toddler who had fallen into a vat of mint ice cream.

'Good morning, Inspector Yard,' said Ms. Wap and Stonewall together, their secateurs and blowlamps at present arms.

'We rather feared you were out for the count'

'I trust you are concussion free this bright and triumphal morning.'

'Spectacular', assures Yard. 'He that laughs last sleeps hardest. I feel like a million for that little nap.'

'Seems we have assembled a team that is more than adequate for the task.'

'Quickly,' says Ms. Wap, 'there being no time to lose we must establish some procedures.'

'How about this,' says Yard. 'You take the high lobe and I'll take the low lobe and I'll be on Gardeners' Question Time afore ye.'

'I intend to isolate the heart of this giant weed, and lay it bare. Once it has been disabled, commandoes will chopper in a bevy of Daikon AirCon's MicroJaz Koolas — small, portable yet amazingly powerful units, designed with the needs of hikers and mountaineers in mind, but suitable for travelling salesman, the residentially challenged, and nomads. These little beauts — a dozen or two is all they will need — will cool the rhizome, slowing down its metabolism and stalling further activity until that chap gets back from the depot with the paraquat.'

'Or,' ventured Yard, 'we could just hack it to a messy pulp and shovel it down the toilet. But whatever we do, let's get on with it, this is my day for shampooing the commissioner.'

'Do you think we should begin with no further ado?' asked Stonewall for clarification.

'An excellent idea,' chuckled Yard. 'You should be a middle manager.' And without ceremony he took a massive swipe with his machete at the big round flanks of the bulb and missed. As Yard spins helplessly on his axis, Stonewall and Wap are able to see that Yard missed because the rhizome had abruptly and without preamble plunged through the floor.

The Heavenly Estate had been designed and built decades previously with the intention of accommodating nothing heavier than a nuclear family. When calculating stress loads the designers had not factored in huge potatoey globes of rhizome, tons of writhing vegetation or elephantine detectives. And since the estate was built with taxpayers' money, the contractors had felt obliged to reinterpret the specs and made the decking a smidgeon smaller and thinner — and the walls a bit hollower and flimsier, the girders a micro-tad less rigid and a mite less than completely bolted on — than requested. Happily, what was lost in stability and safety was more than recouped in the contractor's profit margins.

The short of it is, confronted with so many unfactored-in factors, and being required to do so many things they hadn't been made for, the floor decided it must have been mistaken in its belief in itself as a floor in the first place. If it were a floor it would be doing floor-like things, such as supporting nuclear families and tasteful mock Louis XIV cabinets. Asked now to perform unfloor-like tasks such as supporting unreasonably large vegetable masses, it decided that it could not possibly be a floor after all. If it wasn't a floor, it had no idea what it actually was and in the immediate region of the root thing speculatively ceased to be. The sudden local absence of floor sent the rhizome to the floor below, which, seeing the sense in it's senior's decision, leapt immediately and with commendable resolve to the same decision to cease to be — and so too the many floors below when the vegetable arrived there. Without floors to hem, a great many of the walls found themselves suddenly without raison d'etre and gave up being walls.

In being asked to be something that it wasn't, and therefore ceasing to be, the stuff of Nirvana Heights was in very much the same predicament as the being that had ceased to be and had become a huge cheese plant.

The alert reader will be aware that the helplessly gyrating Yard is one of those things the estate's designers had negligently failed to account for in their plans and the floor. Very satisfied with its decision that the middle part should cease to be, now, with the enthusiasm of one who had finally found meaning in life, ceased to be all over, tipping Yard and Stonewall and Ms. Wap and Weed's mould into the maelstrom of collapsing things below.

Outside, the massed ranks of Parks and Benches operatives and riot police, who had been forced to retreat all the way back to the fringes of the estate by the growing thingy, were surprised to see a lot of dangling weed apparently being sucked back through the upper windows of Nirvana Heights at great speed only to explode and billow a second later from the lower windows of the building with a lot of dust and existentially bothered masonry.

The dust settles like dispersing morning mist in a jungle — albeit, the kind of morning mist that leaves everything dry and powdery.

Nothing moves.

Surely, figure the Parks and Benches operatives, whatever it was in there was done for in that implosion and can they go home now? Nirvana Heights has been hollowed out. All the floors, the walls, the stuff and nonsense of thousands of flats piled on top of each other now lie in a different, less organised pile.

The outer walls still stand to create a vast towering hall whose ceiling, so far up, is lost in the dark. White girders of morning light etch a new architecture within the walls. Long, tangled skeins of vegetation dangle from the windows and the jutting stumps of concrete beams. Water drips, gushes and falls from broken pipes. It is quite beautiful — as long as the entirely innocent families that lived here get proper compensation for their ruined stuff. A few pigeons are already flapping around, evaluating the place as a venue for egg laying or a toilet. It seems the ugly old tower block has been converted into a place to lie down and listen to ambient music.

But the rustling of leaves and feathers and the gentle ethereal sploshing of water and the peace cannot last long.

Here lies unfinished business and unstill minds. Deep within the rubble there's a profound intestinal churning. Things slide off the pile and the churning turns to a rumbling. It is either an earthquake or, slightly more likely in this non-quakey part of the world, it is Yard extracting himself from the pile. And there he is, barging his way up into the light like Godzilla emerging from the flanks of Mt. Fuji and greeting the world with a cheery and bellicose, 'Hi, honey, I'm home!'

He heads off up the mountain, shaking off dust and chunks of masonry. Yard may have may have laboured on foot up the equivalent of a small mountain and through dense jungle, he may have had a man dropped on his head, he may have then been dropped the height of the same small mountain, and been buried in concrete rubble but he was yet a man with a mission.

The object of the mission lies at the peak of this wreckage here: there sits the rhizome slightly atilt in a bed of leaves at the peak of the mound like a meringue atop a very decadent dessert. Over teeth of stone and blades of steel, Yard's big soft shoes crunch comfortably as if walking over nothing more testing than a big pile of cornflakes. He is in a no-more-Mr.-Nice-Guy kind of mood, and murders with his bare hands any bits of the weed that come within arm's reach.

And as he climbs he goes through his mantra of revenge: 'That's for all the spinach they put on my plate at school.' Yank. 'That's for all the lettuce they put in my hamburgers.' Slash. 'That's for all the cabbage they put in my sauerkraut.' Tear. 'That's for all the salad they put on my slugs.' Hack.

Until he comes within lurching distance of his rotund but inert enemy, where he couldn't resist the briefest of victory songs.

Humpty Rhizome sat on a wall,
Humpty Rhizome had a great fall.
All the King's horses and all the King's men

Kicked Humpty's head in again and again.

But it is not Yard's lucky day. Yodelling like an English drunk on an alpine holiday and swinging from a long hairy vine in a cultural clash equalled in horror only by his pink, purple and puce shell suit, Warren appears from the dark distance. Yard has to wait impatiently for warren to touch down between him and the thingy because Warren's dramatic singing, yodelling appearance was accompanied by much twisting and swinging in the wrong direction.

'This is getting monotonous', mutters the policeman.

'It's all right for you, you're not the one hanging about,' retorts Warren.

Yard barges into Warren like a thirsty old drunk trying to get to the bar in a very crowded pub.

Warren is swept immediately off the crest of the hill and down the far side. It is clear where this little bout is going: it's going right out the door and down the street.

'Hold up, hold up, hold up,' says Warren. 'My knickers are in a twist.'

Yard the humanitarian halts. Under the circumstances he feels it reasonable that his foe should be vanquished with at least the dignity of comfortable underpants, and displays of mercy on the edge of total victory only rub the loser's nose in it more. Warren rummages quickly not wanting to keep the nice policeman waiting too long.

'Don't get lost in there,' says Yard. 'You're not thinking of disappearing up your own escape tunnel are you?'

'Got to mind I don't get bitten by this huge snake in here', says Warren apologetically and fishes out of a linty fold the thing he has been looking for. It is a large medicinal looking object, which, while Yard is still distractedly thinking up jokes about underpants and bottoms, he flips like a peanut into the air and catches in his mouth. It is Warren's fourteenth black bomber of the day and he hangs on for dear life as Yard barrels into him like a locomotive. Warren braces himself, his splayed and locked feet bulldozing wreckage and foliage behind him until something in the mess locks solid and the pair come to a halt.

Yard looks straight at Warren, the features of his face frantically scurrying about into grins of comprehension, smirks of shock and happy frowns of loin girding. Then he finds himself in sliding, impotent retreat. He looks down at his feet to check they haven't gone into reverse by themselves, but they really are just sliding along the ground. Warren snarls, all livid yellow teeth and purple lips and puts every ounce of narcotically enhanced strength into the shove.

Now Yard's braced legs, short and pneumatic like the buffers at the end of a railway line, are pushing a huge pile of debris and plant and he thinks he is going back and back and completely out of the picture. Then his splayed stumps find purchase and he's off again, pushing and puffing like a psychotic Thomas the Tank Engine.

And back and forth they go, shoulders locked against each other, turning the rubble pile mountain into a crater, turning the rhizome's high dais into a deep amphitheatre.

Outside, the advancing squares of police and operatives are sent reeling back in disarray as dislodged masonry hurtles out the windows at them and the ground begins to shake. The shaking turns to a rattlin' and then a rollin', leaving everyone in the city dancing like rock n' roll loonies just to stay on their feet.

The two men struggle on, diplomatically taking it in roughly equal turns to be the pusher and the pushed as the quaking thunders on and the sun turns black, pouring molten night on the bewildered city and bolts of lightning are knocked from a cloudless sky; it rained frogs, it rained locusts, it rained sardines, it rained gerbils, and hard-bitten advertising executives became devout Buddhists.

This goes on until insurance underwriters everywhere are packing for Rio, and until Warren finds what he has been looking for: an exit, a hole big enough to drive an entire Yard through. So now here they come locked together as if one, out of Nirvana heights into the

Nuremberg plazas of the estate and on and on, Yard's feet without purchase squealing on the concrete and blowing up gouts of smoke as the Tarmac melts with the friction. Behind and above him a grey-green wave of rubble and weed churning and cresting and breaking, sweeping up fleeing police officers, Parks and Benches operatives, journalists, residents; sweeping them up with shopping trolleys, cars, skips and dog poo, then depositing them in the turbulent wake of our Titans like small bits of wriggling flotsam or very disoriented prawns.

Suddenly Yard's skidding feet lock on something in the rubbish — a curb or a crevice or a sleeping policeman. The two come to a mantle-splitting halt, and grapple on to decide who plays loco next while the estate reels under them. Their foreheads and glares are pressed together with enough power and sweat to put the sharpest crease in the most recalcitrant trousers.

But what is this? Yard has broken eye contact and is staring elsewhere, and the power of his shove eases a bit. Here he is, in the middle of a titanic struggle to save civilisation as we know it and the good inspector isn't paying attention.

Yard steps sideways out of Warren's embrace, leaving his adversary to topple helplessly into a deep, soft pile of the thingummy.

Yard is looking at Ermintrude, who has been driven away from fertilizing duties in the strange old man's flat by all the invading green stuff that is getting along famously with all the green stuff that was already there. She wears sun goggles to protect her eyes from the UV lamp in the old man's odd windowless conservatory, but she shakes these free from her head to better return Yard's rapt gaze.

'Can it be?' asks Yard. Tears dribble from Ermintrude's big black eyes.

'Oh my good gawd!' exclaims the lachrymose plod. 'Mummy!'

They waddle rapidly over to each other and Yard picks up the cow in a big dopey hug. He turns, still cradling the beast in his arms, and as Ermintrude nuzzles his cheeks — which is a lot of nuzzling for a day — he walks slowly and happily out of the estate and down the High Street, heading west toward the Sunset Bar, cooing and burbling to his long lost mother. Yard and Ermintrude are now replete with the sense of belonging and affection that should belong to everyone. Yard no longer has to invent a sense of worth with excesses of authority and no longer needs to seek and test approval with a torrent of crap jokes. Ermintrude no longer needs to become a pile of hamburgers.

And Warren no longer needs to remain awake. Finding he is sitting on one of his undrunk beers from the night before, he jabs his finger through the tab, necks the whole lot, belches mightily and passes out in a big cushiony nest of leaves.

Back on the Heavenly Estate, Sergeant Testosteroni is having the devil of a job locking up his Alpha Squad. He also has a terrific migraine. The two things are not unrelated. He is having a job because every time he gets near the lock with the key, the entire vehicle jolts or jumps or skids or slides a bit closer to Nirvana heights. Seems it is being dragged away by the thingy. Stealing police property — another crime to add to the thingy's impossibly long list, which is properly detailed in his little black book.

Catching up with the escaping armoured car is becoming a serious effort, requiring that Testosteroni climb over unstill drifts of tangled roots. Golf ball globes of sweat and grease cover his head and he is getting closer to Nirvana Heights while everyone else is getting as far away as possible. The earthquake and the explosion type things from inside the tower block have shaken out the weed so that it now covers the whole estate and is rapidly escaping into the adjacent streets.

Huge roots with the girth of old trees have nose-dived through the concrete and slithered into the clay and rock beneath the city. Smaller roots have exploited drains and cracks in the paving or left-ajar pantry doors to find nourishment. The thingy seemed to be growing at a ravenous rate and the forces deployed to contain it have been scattered.

Reg, the parks and benches operative and humanity's last hope, did finally return from the depot with his paraquat, but no one was able to get the lid off the tin. The police and the Parks and Benches operatives established a prising team whose first effort with a long screwdriver and two pairs of knees sent the can spinning, still closed, into the darkest recesses of the thingy's folds and forever beyond use.

Helicopters whump overhead but look like speculative dragonflies and the sun beams down like huge mischievous twinkle in a big blue eye. Under the sun, the leaves and fronds of the thingy are stood upright and chatting and nodding and nudging each other in mass approval of the warm breeze and the sparkling light while kids leap and bound among the most flung and temerarious regions, daring it on and slashing it to bits with sticks, bike chains, tyre levers, Stanley knives, and flame throwers improvised from hair spray cans and lighter refills.

The adults hang back exercising grim expert opinions about the nature and import of the thing. It is a product of genetic engineering, it is science gone wrong; it is God's punishment for something or other; it is criminal negligence on the part of the local authorities; it is terrorism or bio-terrorism or vegetable warfare; it is a complete and utter mystery; it *makes you think, dunnit*. The kids have got it figured out for what it really is: it is fun.

Testosteroni, upside down on an especially steep bank of root, wondered whether it really mattered that the Alpha

Squad's doors were unlocked seeing that it was about to be devoured by a huge omnivorous cheese plant. He thought he might give up trying to lock the doors but the thought went against all his training and provoked several stony, fat and growling beings in his head to shout and threaten and berate him for even thinking about it. But their protestations seemed to go very much against material objective reality as he was experiencing it so he thought he might tell these dour megalomaniacs to go to hell and leave him to sort things out as he saw best, and he was right, because he did, and his migraine went away immediately.

Weedilogue

And Lo! As the sun rolled down the slope of the sky to clunk in the tray beyond the hills where all the other suns have collected like a drawer full of lost marbles, news came of a second weedy thing. A large growth, as rampant and mysterious as the first, was fast consuming a suburb all the way across town from the Heavenly Estate.

And as with the first one, there doesn't seem to be an awful lot anyone could do to stop it.

Under the baleful eyes of the cops and the city fathers, the Parks and Benches operatives, all pooped out from their terribly early start to drinking tea, went home to bed. They could just as well start again at dawn on double time, and flex off when the job was done or when they felt like it, whichever came first.

Eventually, dawn rose greenly. During the night the two plants, the two wotsits, had consumed the city. Where once there were vistas of grey and concrete or bold, thrusting edifices to commerce, or wildly jazzing lights that made people want to spend money and proud if tortuous processions of sexy technology, there was a canopy of green, bursting clouds of foliage and flocks of exotic birds. Who knows, there may be anacondas and jaguars lurking in there. The city dwellers had a new world to explore without even leaving.

The plant things met on the banks of the river where they lay much entwined like two long-lost lovers. Their boughs crossed and embraced, their vines coiled round each other as if writing their own Kama Sutra, their fruit pressed against each other and even squeezed a few juices.

People waited for their morning buses in green arbours, for their trains in moley tunnels full of roots. Toucans and parakeets flapped and screeched. The stalled commuters were for once unconcerned about the non appearance of their transport and plucked avocadoes and exotic fruit from the vines for breakfast. And they ate with their hands and juice dribbled down their arms and they smiled sweetly at each other.

The city's cats were having wonderful time pretending to be tigers in a forest and chasing shadows and butterflies.

And how quiet it was. Not a car or lorry or advertising jingle to be heard. Only, perhaps, the odd Tarzan-like cry in the distance. If you turned on the telly, all you got was pictures of leaves and branches swaying gently in a pleasant breeze.

Not much happened at Daikon AirCon that day. The consumption of the city by two enormous cheese plants was one even for which even the best trainees had no contingency plan.

Slater Stonewall and Ms. Wap would have to re-write the training manual but neither came into the office. They were always there — in spirit if not in body. Where could they be?

They were, as it happened, not far away. They were on the roof. Or on various rooves, whichever elevated point took their fancy from minute to minute. Stonewall had abandoned his crisp suit for a loincloth. Ms. Wap had given up her corporate togs for a loincloth of her own and a boob cloth to go with it.

In the green and the invigorating oxygen, they had found each other or found themselves, or found both themselves and each other simultaneously, and crying like Tarzan and Jane, they swing together through the forest on vines, pausing once in a while at the choicest fruit which they pluck bare handed and offer each other. Sometimes their hands grasp the same piece of fruit at the same time, and they eat it together, eyes locked, mouths getting closer and closer through the soft flesh. Sometimes they just stop and shag. The spray of vines is like a canopy on a huge bridal bed.

Way down below, we find Inspector Yard, as naked as the day he was born, suckling Ermintrude the cow. Ermintrude is very happy — they both are. She is delighted to have found her son and dotes on him. She nuzzles him till he gurgles with delight. She chews her cud and shares it with him.

Warren reclined on a high branch with the sun on his face. He wondered where he could get a proper sausage breakfast, some booze and some fags. Not that he was overly bothered. But, you know, it would be handy if that sort of stuff grew on trees.

There was a rustling in the foliage around him. A big rustling. A rustling more appropriate to something big, like gorillas or mastodon than to leaves. Something large was on the move and it wasn't Warren's.

It was coming from below — branches heaved and shifted to let it through. It turned out to be a red sports car of the open-topped variety that Warren particularly drooled for and it contained, unless Warren was very much mistaken, a case of champagne, several cartons of his brand of cigarettes, and a startled woman who was blond and wore the shirt of his football team.

'Ooh, Warren,' she exclaimed. 'I had such a start!'

'Sharon!' Warren exclaimed with his own start.

'I just got knocked into this car thing and whisked up here. What is going on?

Warren scrutinised the wotsit, the weed, in as many directions as his head would allow.

'You little ...' he said with a big grin.

'Funny thing,' Sharon said, 'is I was just thinking of you ...'

'You was?'

Sharon looked very sheepish.

'To be honest, I was looking for you ... I can't believe I'm saying this! But with the wotsit and all it seemed silly not too.'

Neither could Warren believe it, but he was willing to expand his mind to accept the concept. He had for a long time adored Sharon from afar.

'The truth is,' said Sharon, 'I have for a long time adored you from afar. Aagh! Now I've done it!'

She had, indeed.

'Er, sorry, love,' said Warren. 'The thing is I'm totally focussed on my career. Upwardly mobile. Climbing the ladder, I am. Committed to a life of asceticism and optimised outcomes. I am dedicating my energy and talents to spreading the gospel according to Daikon on every known continent, bringing the dignity and peace of mind that only air conditioners can provide in a focussed and effective manner, as such. I have abnegated my actual self to The Mission Statement, innit.'

'Oh,' said Sharon still in the back seat of the car in her football shirt. 'That isn't even a little bit awkward. Well, erm, that's that then, I suppose.'

'But tell you what,' said Warren gravely. 'I think I could possibly consign all that the bin labelled bollocks and have a life instead.' And he bounded with considerably less grace than Rudolph Valentino into the car where he and Sharon spent the day chasing each other round the seats, drinking champagne and etcetera.

Eventually they collapsed, all shagged out, in the back seats and lay in each other's arms, saying nothing and just thinking green thoughts.

Warren noticed something a little odd. Today he had noticed lots of odd things, but he thought he might as well notice one more.

A spray of branches nearby was carrying a fruit that was not banana or lychee or avocado. It was carrying something that looked remarkably like cooked sausages.

Warren reached out without disturbing Sharon and plucked one of the sausage things and tasted it. Sausage it was, and very tasty too. Not your common-all-garden variety. Warren was impressed.

'Ah,' he said to himself. 'My umbrageous little sausage tree.'

And that was that.

Also by Chris Page

Another Perfect Day in Fucking Paradise

Ben seems to be the only living person on the planet and the dead are really getting on his nerves.

But then he discovers he may not be alone.

Can Ben find love among the dead or will death find him first?

Another Perfect Day in Fucking Paradise is the fifth novel (or first novella) from Chris Page and is a blend of high farce and low horror.

Sanctioned

Are you dead weight?

Britain is sinking under the weight of scroungers, skivers, shirkers, refugees, migrants, libtards and experts. The economy is hobbled and the very fabric of society is in need of a good scrubbing. Gideon Smith, an agent of the Department of Aspiration, has been tasked with doing something about it — and in no uncertain terms.

King of the Undies World

Victoria Gousset, rich, beautiful, daft, and heir to an improbably massive fortune, has been kidnapped.

Her father, mercurial underwear magnate Sir Hades Gousset, sees a way to make capital from the kidnap of his daughter and sets his own cunning plan in motion.

Persephone Gousset, volcanic wife of Hades, discovers her husband's ruse to exploit his daughter's predicament and hatches her own plot to teach her scheming husband a lesson.

The farcical collision of these events propels Victoria on a misadventure that takes her across continents and beyond, while catapulting the Goussets, their friends and enemies into a series of catastrophes that eventually threaten the destruction of the planet.

And all because of some pants.

King of the Undies World is the first volume of the Underpants of Fire trilogy in which Sir Hades, Victoria and Persephone pursue adventures in underwear.

"Apparently this is the first in a trilogy, great news if that's true because I thoroughly enjoyed this one and could easily go another two books.

"Underpants, millionaires, North Koreans, rats, kidnapping and sticky buns, this book has everything a true comedy book should have."
      — Damon Mckinlay, writing on Amazon

The Underpants Tree

Whoever controls underwear controls the world!

Sir Hades Gousset — underwear magnate, king of the undies world, the biggest man in pants — has only ever seen underwear as a force for good. That is, until the mysterious Dr Hieronymus Mangler appears with a fiendish new technology that threatens Hades' monopoly and his grip on the world of nether-wear.

Mangler's technology has more sinister purposes than business competition and his ambitions go beyond mere financial profit. The battle between Hades and Mangler for control of this vital undergarment becomes a titanic struggle for the soul of humanity itself, and leads to not just one, but two apocalypses, in a conflict that rocks civilisation to its foundation wear.

The Underpants Tree is the second volume of The Underpants of Fire trilogy. The first volume is King of the Undies World.

"Thank-you for making my days funnier and reminding me that laughter really is the best medicine. Loved the book!"
— Anna Yamato, writing on Facebook

Un-Tall Tales

Un-Tall Tales is a collection of short fiction, poetry, flash fiction and odds and ends.

In 'The Freebie', musical wannabe Billy Freeb's fifteen minutes are upon him. Will he survive?

The poems explore underpants, teeth, chickens, and tombstones. Will literary sensibility survive?

'Cats Die' relates how our hero decides to combat the crisis of middle age by having an affair with a teenage girl. Will he survive?

The hero of 'Dumb Novel' achieves literary fame for a book he didn't write. Will he survive?

'Escapology' — on a whim, the hero has himself chained, locked in a box and dropped through a hole drilled in the Arctic ice cap. Will he survive?

'Bog' is a bloggy rumination on sausages and twigs. Will the human attention span survive?

Before you go …

And finally — please support your local struggling artist (without spending any more money)

If you've read and enjoyed a book by Chris Page or any other independent author, please consider giving it a star rating and/or review on Amazon and/or Goodreads. These ratings really do help. They raise the title in the rankings and reassure potential readers that the story is not actually toxic or liable to cause injury.

The author thanks you in advance.

Find out more on these sites

chris-page.com

psipook.com

weedthenovel.com

www.ingramcontent.com/pod-product-compliance
Lightning Source LLC
Chambersburg PA
CBHW060926120626
46557CB00003B/888